THE YEAR IS 1987 . . .

Americans are discovering a new patriotism and a concern for the environment. There's a mini baby boom as women of every age are having babies, combining family and career—and finding the Superwoman Syndrome more than it's cracked up to be. Farm Aid and Live Aid incite people everywhere to help out—even yuppies, with their "upwardly mobile" material life-style. Reagan leads the country into a New Traditionalism, and Gorbachev fires the world's imagination.

The red power suit is the business fashion of the day for women, while every man on Wall Street sports a yellow tie and suspenders. Mousse is essential for those high-flying, gravity-defying hairstyles.

Michael Jackson popularizes moonwalking—the kind done on planet Earth, while Patrick Swayze's *Dirty Dancing* inspires couples everywhere to learn the steamy seduction of the merengue.

It is a time of pride in America, and of concern for the conservation of our world.

It is a time of reaching out, at home and across the globe, to welcome new friends.

It is the time of Abby Fielding and Aleksandr Rostov.

Dear Reader,

This month, our nostalgic journey through the twentieth century brings us to 1987, for A Century of American Romance's *My Only One*.

The prolific Eileen Nauman tells the dramatic tale of a love between an American marine biologist and a Soviet naval officer whose hope for the success of *glasnost* is more than a hope for world peace.

Next month, watch for the final title in A Century of American Romance—*A > Loverboy,* Judith Arnold's lighthearted look at love in 1998. It's a glimpse into the future you won't want to miss.

We hope you've been enjoying these special stories of nostalgia. As always, we welcome your comments. Please take the time to write to us at the address below.

Here's hoping A Century of American Romance becomes part of your most cherished memories....

Sincerely,

Debra Matteucci
Senior Editor & Editorial Coordinator
Harlequin Books
300 East 42nd St.
New York, NY 10017

EILEEN NAUMAN

1980s
M Y
O N L Y
O N E

Harlequin Books

TORONTO • NEW YORK • LONDON
AMSTERDAM • PARIS • SYDNEY • HAMBURG
STOCKHOLM • ATHENS • TOKYO • MILAN

To Nina Gettler, my dear Russian friend who
wisely counseled me out of and around the
stereotypes in order to get to the soul and
heartbeat of a wonderful people. Thank you,
Dushinka.

AND

To Mikhail Gorbachev, a Russian who not only
speaks of change, but makes it a reality for all
people of this world.

AND

To Peace on Earth.

Published April 1991

ISBN 0-373-16385-1

MY ONLY ONE

Chapter One

April 1987

"Comrade Captain, the Japanese catcher ship and American salmon trawler are going to collide!"

Second Captain Aleksandr Rostov twisted around in the nylon seat in the rear of the Soviet Helix helicopter. The gray-green water of the Bering Sea lay one thousand feet below them.

Craning his neck, Alec could see a huge Japanese factory ship, followed by a secondary whaling fleet of ten smaller vessels, known as "catchers," shadowing a pod of humpback whales swimming in a northward direction. He saw the metal harpoon on the bow of one of the catchers aimed at the closest whale, not quite within range to shoot—yet.

"Comrade Captain, do you see them...?"

Lieutenant Yuri Mizin was obviously upset. The earphones in Alec's helmet hissed, blotting out the rest of the pilot's observation. But Alec could see Zotov, the helicopter crewman, excitedly jabbing a gloved finger at the Plexiglas window behind him.

Alec's eyes narrowed. Mizin hadn't dramatized the situation below them. One lone American trawler flying a Save Our Whales Foundation flag from the mast was brazenly challenging the path of the large, powerful catcher ship.

"Are they fools?" Alec said to no one in particular as Mizin dropped the helicopter to a lower altitude.

Mizin's laugh was a bark. "Crazy Americans! Comrade Captain, didn't you hear our radios picking up talk between the Americans and the Japanese whaling fleet since yesterday?"

"Off and on." Most of the time he'd been busy in his office on board the *Udaloy,* not on the bridge.

He'd left the destroyer half an hour ago, for a quick hop to a Soviet cruiser forty miles south of their position. An Izvestia reporter doing an unheard-of story about officers in the naval fleet wanted to interview Alec in his position as the *Udaloy*'s navigation officer. Perhaps Alec's study of communications had prompted the fleet commander to choose him. Whatever the reason, Alec surmised that with *glasnost* and *perestroika* becoming the new watchwords in the Soviet Union, this interview was all part of the new openness wanted by Moscow.

Alec had taken the fleet commander's order to fly to the cruiser with good grace, even though it seemed so frivolous in comparison to his usual demanding duties. Now, though, he feared he was about to find himself in the midst of an incident.

"The trawler has been shadowing this fleet for the past five days," Mizin explained. "First Captain Denisov wanted to make sure the Japanese didn't fish in our two-hundred-mile economic-limit territory. That's why we've been paralleling the whaling fleet, to remind them to remain in international waters. Yesterday afternoon this American trawler burst over the horizon and started breaking up the pods of humpback whales so the Japanese catcher ships couldn't start harpooning them."

Alec recalled Captain Denisov, his commander, saying something about the shadowy trawler because Alec had had to plot several different courses as a result. He watched the tiny trawler, partly rusted out and resembling more of a scow than a seaworthy craft, dip up and down like a cork in the eight-foot waves. The Bering Sea was not kind to ships at any time of year, but in late April, the sea was fickle and moody, just like some of the women he'd known during his naval career. A slight smile hovered around Alec's thinned mouth. Not that any woman wanted her husband at sea for six or nine months out of each year. His friend Misha Surin from the Politburo had long ago dubbed him with the nickname of Lone Wolf.

"Lieutenant, is there a Coast Guard vessel nearby in case these ships collide?" Alec had been transferred from the Baltic Command in January, and his only experience with these kinds of incidents was hearsay. He did know, though, that it wasn't wise for the trawler to brawl with a Japanese catcher fifteen times its size.

"*Nyet,* Comrade Captain. I'm worried. Transmissions from the Japanese factory ship indicate the captain has made it clear he will *not* order his catcher ship to turn aside if the American comes across his bow again. He intends to have his catchers shoot the whales or else."

"I see." The crewman handed Alec a pair of binoculars. When he found the trawler, Alec's eyes widened. There, on the wet, slippery deck, was a woman in a bright orange survival suit. Her fiery-red hair was like a flaming banner about her shoulders as she raced toward the bow of the small ship. She was waving her arms madly at the approaching Japanese vessel.

"Little fool," he muttered. "Lieutenant, you said there was no sight of the Coast Guard?" Normally, if an American ship was in trouble, the U.S. Coast Guard would be called to effect rescue. However, the trawler was above the Aleutian Island chain and the closest station was on Kodiak Island, too far away.

"That's correct, Comrade Captain." Mizin hesitated, and then said, "Er…what if they collide? The trawler is small and obviously in poor condition. That catcher ship may well cut it in half. Should I radio the *Udaloy* and alert First Captain Denisov of the situation?"

Denisov was the senior officer aboard the *Uda-loy,* and Alec normally never made command decisions involving anything but navigation-related items. He was, however, senior officer aboard the small helicopter. His hands tightened around the binoculars as he watched the gallant little trawler continue on a collision course with the Japanese whaler. "There have been many of these dramas played out between them," Alec muttered to the pilot. "The Japanese have *never* rammed an American vessel."

"Comrade, you didn't hear the earlier radio transmissions. The Japanese captain on the factory ship is furious. He's behind on his quota and low on fuel. They're hungry for a kill and won't stand for any foolishness from these whale activists. I think they'll ram the trawler if it's foolish enough to get in the way."

Alec couldn't tear his gaze from the woman who now stood in the bow of the trawler. Thick white spume from the sea shot upward, spraying her each time the trawler dipped into a trough. From this distance, he couldn't make out her features, except that she was tall and had red hair that now waved across her shoulders like a crimson flag proclaiming war. "More like a red cape being waved at an angry bull," he said to no one in particular.

"Eh, Comrade Captain?"

"Nothing, Lieutenant." Alec noticed Mizin had brought the Helix into a slow, large circle above the two foreign ships. Apparently the lieutenant took the Japanese threat as real. Alec's mind raced with potentials. The Soviets never interfered in such circumstances. But then, these fights had never bloodied anyone's nose before, either. Did the red-haired Valkyrie on the bow realize how dangerous a situation she was in?

"Lieutenant, I want you to remain on station and use the helo's nose camera to photograph the confrontation." Alec didn't want to be dressed down by Captain Denisov if these two ships collided. Bad press was something General Secretary Gorbachev wanted to avoid at all costs. In the past, Alec knew the Soviets were sometimes blamed simply because they were in the vicinity where trouble erupted. They had been innocent, but the world press leapt at Mother Russia's throat to make them look evil. It was his responsibility to stop incidents such as this from blackening their already tarnished image.

"Yes, sir."

"And call the *Udaloy*. Apprise Captain Denisov of the situation. Ask what his orders are. If that Japanese catcher is stupid enough to make good its threat, that trawler may sink before anyone can get to it. If the captain wants us to become involved, ask him to alert the sickbay staff to prepare to receive injured crewmen." That way, Alec knew his head was off the chopping block. The Soviet navy rarely helped anyone else in distress, but the laws of the open sea permitted offering aid when appropriate.

Glasnost and *perestroika* were underway, and he saw them as an opportunity, a positive one, if Denisov would allow him to orchestrate it properly. For once, the Soviets might be the hero, not the villain.

"Yes, sir."

Mizin continued to circle the Helix downward, and Alec was able to focus on the woman at the bow. Unconsciously, he held his breath. Her hair was long and thick, like a horse's silky mane. But it was her face that made his pulse quicken in an uncharacteristic beat. She reminded him of a fox, her features clean and sharp. Her forehead was broad, with slightly arched eyebrows framing narrowed eyes. He wished momentarily that he were close enough to see their color. Was she the daughter of the sea or the air? Would her eyes be green or blue? He laughed at his romantic side, which he normally kept carefully closeted from the military world, though his curiosity ate away at his frivolous wondering.

Perhaps it was her mouth, set with challenge, or that slender, oval face with that small chin jutting outward that intrigued him most. There was no apology in any line of her body, her fist raised over her head at the approaching catcher that dwarfed her.

Little Fox, you are in great danger. That bear of a Japanese ship will crush you. A fox never takes on a bear. A bear always wins. Lowering the binoculars, Alec frowned. His straight black eyebrows drew together momentarily. Puzzled that a woman he didn't even know could create such a powerful, unbidden response in him, Alec sat there digesting the discovery.

"That Japanese whaler isn't going to back off!" Mizin cried out, swinging the Helix around so that they could fully view the coming collision.

"Any word from Captain Denisov, yet?" Alec snapped, getting out of the nylon-webbed seat and moving forward, hunkering between the pilot and copilot's seats.

"*Nyet*. They'd best hurry with an answer."

As he gripped the back of the two seats, Alec's scowl deepened. "Lower, Comrade. I want that Japanese catcher to be fully aware of our presence. Perhaps he'll back down if he realizes there is a witness to his premeditated murder."

Mizin deftly swung the Helix to the starboard and dropped it to three hundred feet. "I can fly up to his bridge windows."

Alec tendered a tense smile. Mizin would do exactly that—the pilot known for taking chances. "*Nyet,* Comrade. This will do." Why hadn't the captain of the *Udaloy* answered them? Didn't Denisov realize time was limited? In another few minutes, the collision would occur. Placing one knee on the cold metal deck, Alec lodged his shoulders between the pilots' seats to steady himself as he watched the unfolding drama.

"Look at the activity aboard the Japanese ship," Mizin said.

But Alec had the binoculars trained exclusively on the red-haired woman.

His heart picking up in a painful beat, Alec watched mesmerized as the powerful bow of the whaler sliced forward, within a quarter mile of the trawler. "Call the *Udaloy* again! Tell Captain Denisov that a collision is inevitable. I must have an answer *now!*"

"Yes, sir!"

Get out of there, Little Fox! You'll be the first to be killed. Run! Alec's intake of breath was unexpected when the red-haired woman suddenly turned and lifted her face in their direction. Her eyes were a vivid blue, the color of lapis lazuli from Afghanistan. They were filled with the fire of challenge and anger. Alec's mouth stretched into a disbelieving smile. "She's not even afraid. . . ."

He hadn't even realized he'd spoken aloud until it was too late. He was instantly sorry. His comment was completely unmilitary. The woman returned her attention to the catcher. Alec watched in shock as she climbed onto the farthest point on the bow, her arm around the short spike of wood to steady herself in the angry sea. What was she doing? Didn't she realize what was going to happen? Anguish serrated his chest. The sensation was white-hot, galvanizing. Alec froze, the binoculars pressed hard against his eyes, every shortened breath he took, a slicing agony. The red-haired woman would be killed—instantly.

"ABBY! ABBY! THAT JAPANESE ship ain't gonna turn!"

Abby heard the hysteria in the voice of Captain John Stratman across the bullhorn. She turned, watching as the old salmon-fishing captain violently gestured for her to come back to the wheelhouse that was situated amidships the *Argonaut*. The wind was freezing and the spume slapping against the trawler's bow flung upward and drenched her survival suit with the seawater, which instantly froze into a thin coating of ice on her clothing.

Cupping her hand to her mouth she shouted, "No!" The trawler's forward progress increased the windchill factor until her eyes watered with tears.

"He won't turn!" Stratman bellowed. "Get down from there! Get down and prepare for collision!"

Whirling around, Abby clung to the spindly pole on the bow of the *Argonaut*. She shook her gloved fist at the catcher. "I won't let you kill my whales! Turn back!" Her voice cracked with a sob as she watched the black bow raise up and then, in slow motion, come down. Each forward thrust brought them closer and closer. Abby saw the crew of the catcher in the forward turret where the huge, ugly harpoon sat ready for firing at the endangered humpback whales. *Her* whales. The humpback population had been estimated at one hundred fifty thousand at the beginning of the century. Now, less than fifteen thousand were still alive. This pod wasn't going to join those who had already died, not if Abby could help it.

She screamed at the approaching vessel. "You *won't* kill them! You *won't!*" Twisting around, Abby stared at the fleeing pod of whales. The catcher was almost within firing range. The Japanese had never rammed a SOWF vessel or inflatable Zodiac. Never! Captain Stratman was a cautious man, and to this she attributed his terror. The Japanese would never risk an international incident or the bad press resulting in running down a puny trawler. Or would they? It was a David-and-Goliath situation.

Her attention had been snagged by another sound other than the constant roar of the ocean, the laboring chug of the *Argonaut's* pressed engines and the howling wind. She had never seen such an odd-looking helicopter in all her life. It was dark green, with a red star painted on the fuselage. That was right: Captain Stratman had said he'd picked up Soviet ship-to-ship talk this morning. At dawn, she'd seen the ghostly group of what Stratman said were Soviet destroyers shadowing the Japanese whaling fleet.

The helicopter had no weapons visible, so Abby tore her gaze from it and centered her attention on the whaler bearing directly down on them. The Japanese were in international waters and had as much right to be there as the Soviets, and right now were her main concern. For five days she'd dogged the heels of the whaling fleet, disrupting their bid to

kill the pods of humpback whales that came north at
this time of year with their newly born calves from
the Revillagigedo Islands near Baja, Mexico or from
Maui. The Japanese didn't care whether their steel
harpoons punctured the side of a nursing cow, struck
a calf or any other member of the family.

The *Argonaut* crew consisted of only four people,
one a SOWF photographer who was taking photos
of the event, and the other, the first mate to Stratman. Abby saw both men running toward the bridge,
struggling into their life vests. She'd left hers on the
bridge as the survival suit was too bulky anyway.
With a life vest over it, she'd barely be able to turn
or do much of anything. The brackish waves were
growing higher. She clung to her perch on the bow
and continued to wave her fist up at the whaler. The
gesture was a language anyone could interpret, no
matter what country they came from.

Spray slammed up against the *Argonaut,* drench-
ing Abby. The water was chilling, like a slap in the
face. Her long, naturally curly hair was stiff with salt
and frozen to her suit. Wiping her face, she blinked.
It was then she realized with awful clarity that the
catcher wasn't going to turn aside as it had previously. Abby's grip tightened around the pole. She
heard Stratman's cry of warning torn away by the
wind as he jerked the wheel of the *Argonaut* to starboard. The trawler lurched, hung up on a wave.

Her eyes widened enormously as she watched the
tall, knifelike bow of the catcher lift upward. Mouth

dropping open, Abby suddenly realized that when it came down, it would come down on the trawler. She anchored to the spot, stunned with the realization that she was about to be killed.

She crouched, clinging to the pole, turning away as the catcher bow came down upon them. *No! Oh, God, no!*

"No!" ALEC BLURTED. His cry had been utterly spontaneous, but he couldn't help himself. He watched the deadly ballet of the two ships as they slid downward into the same trough of water and collided. At the last second, the trawler had heaved starboard to try to soften the impact of the collision. A cry clawed up Alec's constricted throat and stuck there as he watched the catcher's bow strike the port side of the *Argonaut* in a grazing motion. The violent impact tossed the woman off the bow and high into the air.

Alec dropped the binoculars as he rose, tense and disbelieving, his gaze riveted on the woman. She had struck the water a good fifty feet away, her red hair like a flame against the gray-green sea.

"Rescue her!" Alec snapped to Mizin. "Get down there and get her!"

"But, Comrade Captain," Mizin began helplessly, "Captain Denisov hasn't given us permission to—"

Whirling around in the cramped confines of the Helix, Alec growled, "I'm giving the order, Lieutenant!'' His decision could easily mean an international incident. Alec knew that no one, not even his friend Misha Surin, from the public-affairs office in the Politburo, could save him from being sent to a Siberian labor camp for making this decision solely on his own.

Suddenly, he didn't care. He'd been playing it safe and cautious all his life. This woman, who had displayed such incredible courage, deserved better than a death in the icy sea. She had no life vest, and that survival suit she wore could drag her down into the sea in minutes. If she didn't drown, she would die of hypothermia within thirty minutes.

Zotov quickly slid the door open, and a cold blast of Arctic air filled the confines of the helo. Alec stood tensely at the door as Zotov expertly guided Mizin verbally toward the floundering woman. The pilot dropped the Helix fast, and Alec clung to the air-frame door, his feet spread apart for maximum balance. The wind from the double rotor blades was whipping up the grasping, hungry fingers of the sea all around her.

Alec leaned out the fuselage door, the cold air numbing his features. His eyes widened as he saw blood covering part of the woman's face as she struggled to keep her head above water. ''Quickly!'' he snapped at Zotov. ''Get the collar lowered quickly!''

The bright orange collar was placed on a hoist hook outside the door and lowered. It swung and twirled wildly beneath the Helix, caught in the air turbulence created by the aircraft. Alec leaned out, the blasts from the rotors pummeling his body like punches from a boxing opponent.

Abby couldn't scream, she couldn't even cry out; sea water funneled up her nostrils and then burned down the back of her throat and into her vulnerable lungs. Though she was dazed, the freezing water kept her semiconscious. Awkwardly, she flailed around, the drenched survival suit pulling her downward, always downward.

Barely aware that the Soviet helicopter hovered nearby, Abby struggled weakly. The water was stealing what little heat was left in her body. Her flesh was numb; she felt nothing. *Die . . . I'm going to die,* she thought disjointedly. It was so hard to push upward, to keep her head above the water. The stout leather boots she wore were becoming heavier by the second, constantly tugging at her from below like hands pulling her down into the icy depths.

A huge wave caught her and she cried out. Too late! Water streamed into her open mouth and she went under. Every movement stole more of her eroding strength, but Abby fought back. She broke through to the surface, gagging, and weakly tried to focus on the helicopter now hovering thirty feet above her. Blinking the salt water from her eyes, she saw two men leaning out, lowering something she didn't recognize.

The collar landed ten feet away from her and floated on the water. She looked up to see one man, leaning out of the helo at a dangerous angle and gesturing for her to swim toward the object. Coughing violently, Abby tried, but her arms were leaden. The suit felt like encasing concrete. And the sea was stealing the last of her body heat until no matter what her barely functioning brain screamed at her, the signals just didn't reach her muscles.

"She's going to go down!" Zotov screamed at Alec. "She's too weak to swim to the collar!"

With a curse, Alec watched the woman's waxen features. When her eyes rolled back in her head, he knew she'd lost consciousness. He tore off his helmet, then his parka. There was no time to unlace his heavy black leather boots.

Turning to Zotov, he screamed at him above the roar of the helo, "I'm going to jump. I'll get her to the collar. You lift us both up!"

Zotov nodded jerkily, his eyes huge.

It was a thirty-foot drop into the ocean. Alec's alarm increased as he saw the woman slide beneath the surface for the last time. Taking a deep breath, he leapt from the helo.

Abby's last coherent thought before she surrendered to her watery grave was of the man tearing the clothes from his body. When he removed the helmet, she could clearly see his taut features: a lean, intense face with dark brown eyes that seemed to burn with some undefinable inner light, hair cut military short and the color of the black walnuts that each autumn fell from the trees around her apartment in Alexandra, Virginia. Just the anxiety, the care building in his eyes, made her try one last time when she realized he was stripping off unnecessary clothing to jump out the door to save her.

With the last of her strength, she lifted her hand above her head as the sea jerked her downward. Her icy glove stretched upward in a silent plea of help. It was the last thing she remembered.

Alec landed in the Bering Sea with a huge splash. The icy water tore the breath from him as he shot back up to the surface. Shaking his head in a violent motion to blink away the seawater from his eyes, Alec saw her hand just as it slid beneath the surface. With floundering strokes he reached her, but she was already beneath the water. Gulping in a huge breath of air, he jackknifed into a dive, lunging beneath the surface. There! He saw her red hair floating around her waxen features like living red coral. Kicking hard, he propelled himself downward, his hand outstretched, but the cold was stealing his strength. *If only… if only… There!*

Alec grabbed the shoulder of her survival suit. Instantly, he kicked back toward the surface. To his surprise and terror, the survival suit was much heavier than he'd realized. It took every last vestige of his superb physical condition to get the woman back to the surface. Gasping for air, he placed one arm around her to keep her head up and out of the wa-

ter. Swimming hard for the collar that dangled
nearby, Alec sobbed for breath.

No wonder she'd gone down so quickly. The survival suit felt like an anchor. As hard as Alec kicked,
he realized with a sinking feeling that his boots were
retarding them from reaching the collar. Anxiously,
he glanced at the woman. She wasn't breathing. He
had only minutes to revive her or she'd have permanent brain damage. If he could revive her at all. She
was suffering from hypothermia and a small cut on
her forehead.

The collar, once retrieved, was easy to bring
around himself and the woman. Alec placed both his
arms under her, locking his hands into a fist just below her breasts. He heard the winch begin and instantly felt the collar tighten around them. *Hurry!
Hurry!* The weight from the deadly survival suit was
ponderous. The winch was pulling them up, up, until finally, like two dripping towels being rescued
from the grasping, hungry sea, they slowly came out
of the water.

Alec was nearly beside himself at the slowness of
the winch recovery. Zotov helped him maneuver the
woman into the helo and laid her down on the metal
surface that was glazed over with ice. Alec staggered
into the aircraft on his hands and knees, gasping and
shaking from the cold.

"Shut the door!" he ordered Zotov as soon as he
shrugged out of the collar.

The crewman shut and locked it.

Alec crawled to the woman's side and rolled her onto her belly. Like all officers in the Soviet navy, he'd been taught CPR and advanced first-aid lifesaving techniques. Straddling her, he placed his hands low on her torso and, leaning forward, forced out the water he knew was in her lungs. Zotov hovered nearby. Without a helmet on, Alec was without communications ability with his pilot.

"Get to the *Udaloy!*" Alec yelled above the roar, hoping Zotov would understand him. The crewman jerked a thumbs-up that he understood the order and relayed the command to the pilot. Instantly, the Helix banked right, gained altitude, the engines revving up to maximum pitch.

A half an hour. They had half an hour before Alec could get the woman any kind of medical help. He kept pushing huge amounts of water out of her lungs. Alec was trembling badly, the dark blue one piece suit stuck to his body, icy and stiff. Zotov helped him turn her over on her back.

It was then that Alec got the first good look at her. Her flesh was a bluish gray, indicating she had stopped breathing. With trembling hands, he tore at the zipper of the survival suit. He had to get it off her! It would only impair her chances of surviving, now an icy coffin helping to induce her body into worse hypothermia. Zotov understood. Together, they wrestled with the bulky, wet material, stripping her out of it. Zotov retrieved the thermal recovery capsule and placed her in it.

Why was he doing this? Alec thought. Why was he risking his entire career—his life—for her? He tipped her head back, that mass of red hair spread like a limp halo about her. He saw copper-colored freckles across her cheeks and realized in anguish just how beautifully sculpted her lips really were. Trying to get a pulse at her throat and finding none, Alec knew he must do CPR if he was to even have a chance of saving her.

Even as the helo returned to the *Udaloy*, Alec continued to perform CPR. He tirelessly pumped on her chest to try and get her heart started, and blew his breath into her. He lost track of time, as he always did in an emergency. She became his sole focus, his entire reason for being. As he fitted his mouth to her slack lips, he envisioned not only his breath entering her, but his will for her to live flowing into her slender body at the same time.

Come on, fight back! Do you hear me? Fight back! Where is the fire that shows in your hair? Show it to me! Show it!

Several minutes before Mizin landed the Helix on the aft end of the destroyer, Alec felt a pulse. With a cry of elation, he watched her fine, thin nostrils quiver. He placed his hand on her chest, feeling a trembling, shallow inhalation on her part. He grinned triumphantly up at Zotov, who smiled back. Beneath the survival suit, the woman had worn a heavy pair of white cotton longjohns. They, too, were soaked, but Alec left them on as he and Zotov wrapped her in the thermal capsule once again.

As they landed and the deck crew placed the tie-down chains on the four wheels to stop the Helix from being tossed overboard into the sea, Alec quickly made sure the thermal unit fit snugly around the woman. Her flesh was frighteningly cold, and he knew she would have to be treated immediately for hypothermia. If she wasn't warmed up, her heart would stop beating again.

Zotov jerked the door open. To Alec's relief, two medical corpsmen waited with a stretcher just outside the aircraft. The rotors were slowing, the engine turned off. Alec ignored the curious looks of the sailors and those officers who gathered at a safe distance from the helicopter. With Zotov's help, he transferred the woman to the stretcher and issued orders to have her taken immediately to the dispensary. He followed close behind, soaked to the skin and freezing as never before.

Entering the destroyer from a nearby hatch, Alec was on the heels of the corpsmen. They hurried, lifting their feet high above each hatchway, the passage narrow and confined. What had he done? The ship's captain, Denisov, had never given permission to affect a rescue, much less bring the American woman on board. As cold as Alec was physically, the pit of his stomach tightened considerably—but it was with fear. Fear for his own career for making a decision of this magnitude on his own, without proper authority.

Chapter Two

Alec refused to leave the red-haired woman, choosing instead to wait in Dr. Antoli Ryback's office until she was stabilized. She would have to be stripped out of her wet longjohns, dressed in a cotton gown and then placed back in the thermal capsule in order to slowly elevate her body temperature.

A half an hour later, Ryback ordered Alec into the dispensary. The lean physician stood at the woman's bedside, a scowl on his narrow features as Alec approached.

"Tell me what happened to her out there," he demanded as he placed an IV into her right arm.

In a few succinct sentences, Alec told him. He couldn't tear his gaze from the woman's slack features. She wasn't beautiful, but rather, intriguing looking. Alec forced himself to remain unaffected so that Ryback wouldn't realize his personal interest in her.

"You'd best go see Captain Denisov now. I'm sure he'll want the full story on your heroic rescue effort," Ryback said wryly. "This sounds like a golden opportunity, Comrade."

"Oh?"

"Of course. The Soviets did a good turn for the Americans. You rescued one of their people." He placed the stethoscope against her gowned chest, listening to the woman's lungs, a satisfied expression on his face. "She's going to be fine, so don't look so concerned, my friend. Go, change uniforms and then speak to our captain. I'm sure she'll regain consciousness by the time you return to check on her."

Faintly embarrassed by Ryback's perceptiveness, Alec nodded. As he turned away, he told himself that Ryback was a doctor, therefore more closely attuned to the pulse beat of human actions and reactions. Had his concerns for the woman really been that apparent? As he stepped into the narrow passageway, Alec absently rubbed his chest. Would he return in time to see her awaken? What was her name? Where did she come from? What had possessed her to take on that Japanese catcher? Her courage stunned him. They were but a few of the many questions that plagued Alec as he headed down the passageway deep in thought.

ABBY JERKED AWAKE. Where was she? Where? The room where she was laying was dark except for a red light on the bulkhead, throwing a crimson wash across the small, neatly kept space. Everything was made of metal, except for the curtain beside her bed.

Coughing violently, she pressed her fingers to her raw throat. It was then that she became aware that someone was sitting near her bedside. Abby's eyes widened enormously and her heart pounded unevenly. A man in an unfamiliar uniform was sitting quietly observing her. His eyes held exhaustion and interest in them as he regarded her with a slight, tentative smile. He reached out and turned on a small lamp beside the bed.

"Dr. Abby Fielding?"

She blinked and struggled into a sitting position, feeling dizzy. "Y-Yes?"

"I'm Second Captain Aleksandr Rostov. I want to welcome you aboard the *Udaloy,* a Soviet naval destroyer. Please don't look so frightened. You are our guest. A friend."

Abby stared at him, his words slowly sinking into her spongy mind. "You..." she whispered, her voice choked with emotion, "...you rescued me out there. My God, I thought I was going to die."

Alec slowly rose, not wanting to cause more fear than what was presently mirrored in her lovely blue eyes. "You came very close to death, Doctor." He smiled warmly, trying to disarm her wariness. Her hair lay in wild abandon around her shoulders. She needed to shower to wash the stiff salt brine out of those copper-colored tresses. Placing his hands against the steel tubing around her bed, he added, "Your defiance, your fight, saved you from drowning."

Suddenly emotional because his voice was gentle
with understanding, Abby clung to his dark brown
gaze. "My defiance got me into a collision with that
Japanese catcher. I thought it would turn aside like
it had in previous days, but it didn't." She touched
her throat, the raw feeling uncomfortable. "You
saved my life. I was going down for the count."
Quickly wiping away tears at the corners of her eyes,
she asked, "What about the *Argonaut* crew, Captain? Are they okay?"

"We've got the *Argonaut* in tow behind us. Captain Stratman and the two crew members are staying
on board with a dewatering pump we've loaned
them. The trawler sustained some hull damage and
with our help, they have the leak under control.
They're fine. You were the only one who was injured." When he saw her alarm turn to relief, he
added, "We're taking you to your Coast Guard base
in the Kodiak Islands for repairs. Once we reach the
U.S. twelve-mile limit, a Coast Guard cutter will take
tow of your trawler. At that time, we'll transfer you
to the cutter, too."

"Good...." Abby whispered. "And my whales?
That pod of humpback whales? Did they get away?"

"There is a happy ending for everyone except the
Japanese whaling fleet, who came up with no catch.
Your whales are safe."

Relief cascaded through Abby. When she opened
her eyes, she melted beneath his interested inspection of her. "I'm on board a Soviet ship?"

"Yes. As our guest," Alec stressed.

Suddenly nervous in Alec's presence, Abby nodded. "Thank you so much." She gripped his hand that was resting on the tubing. It was a strong, powerful hand belonging to a man who obviously didn't sit behind a desk any more than necessary. There was an incredible sense of strength about the officer, and yet he was treating her as if she were a frightened child, with gentleness and understanding.

Alec didn't move, the coolness of Abby's fingertips brushing the back of his hand. Her touch had been fleeting. Pulverizing. His heartbeat soared. "Are all Americans like you?" he asked as she removed her hand.

"Like what? Willing to risk their lives for whales?"

His mouth curved into a grin. "Perhaps that also. No, you reached out and touched me. Is that an American thing to do?"

With a little laugh, Abby said, "I'm afraid so." She hesitated. "I should amend that answer. Some of us don't let decorum stand in our way of reaching out and touching a person. Although," she said wryly, "it's more of a western custom than an eastern one."

Cocking his head, Alec absorbed her breathy laughter. Her blue eyes no longer looked dazed. Instead, he discovered gold highlights of amusement in them. "I've never met an American before. You must first forgive me for the endless questions I will ask you. I'm the navigation officer on board, but I studied communications, so my curiosity comes from a personal as well as professional level.''

Abby gasped. "You're a public-relations officer?"

He was shocked by how easily she showed emotion, but oddly, Alec enjoyed the unexpected discovery. "Not exactly."

"Still, you have the background. Then you can help me!"

For the first time in a long time, Alec laughed—fully and deeply. "I doubt many could refuse you, Dr. Fielding."

"Please call me Abby. I can't stand formality."

"I've already gotten that impression. Then you may call me Alec, if you choose."

He had a wonderful name, Abby thought. She liked the dancing highlights in his eyes and his ability to parry her lightning-quick exchanges. "I'd better slow down," she said more to herself than him. "It's my red hair. It's always getting me into trouble." Touching her cheeks, she smiled up at him. "I'd better finish my explanation about Americans being so open and friendly. I've found that people born in the western part of the country are far more friendly and trusting than those born in the east. I was born in La Jolla, California, and where I was raised, it was the thing to do."

"I see. So, reaching out and touching me was a normal thing to do, even though I'm a stranger?"

She made a face. "Well...not every stranger. You have a trusting face. Besides, you saved my life. That should merit a hug of gratitude, too."

For an instant, Alec wanted to suggest something far more intimate. The idea shocked even him, for he had been raised in a very strict, disciplined environment. "I think I like these western people from America," he teased. "Before we go further, how do you feel? Are you hungry?"

Excited about Alec and his friendliness, Abby had forgotten about her own condition. She stopped, took internal stock of herself, and then said, "I'm starving, and I feel fine, except for a sore throat."

"You swallowed a lot of seawater." She had a lovely, long neck, and he ached to reach out and lightly trail his fingers along its length.

Abby said nothing as the experience and the fear came back to her. "I—I almost died."

"Yes," Alec whispered. "A terrible loss if that had happened."

Struck by the emotion in his husky voice, Abby studied his closed, unreadable face. Alec couldn't disguise the feeling in his voice, however, and she allowed his comment to pass without reaction. Clearing her throat, she asked, "Is there any water around? I'm dying of thirst."

"Of course." Alec busied himself getting her a glass of water from the examination room next door. She had suddenly paled when she realized she had almost died. Dr. Ryback had asked Alec to remain

with Abby, the physician hadn't wanted her to wake
up alone in a strange place. Alec had willingly vol-
unteered and had gotten the choice assignment
mainly because he was one of the few men on board
who spoke fluent English. Picking up the phone attached to the bulkhead of the examination room, he
called mess. Letting the chief steward know that he
wasn't going to dine with the other officers as usual,
he then ordered two trays of food to be brought to
the dispensary.

He returned to Abby's bedside and handed her the
large glass of water. She drank the entire contents.
Alec motioned to a small room. "There is a shower
in there. I have food being prepared and brought to
us. Perhaps you would like to clean up before you
eat?"

Abby leapt at his idea. "Yes, I'd love to, thank
you." She wrinkled her nose as she looked down at
the coarse white gown she wore. "I smell awful!"

Unable to stop the smile, Alec released the tubing
from one side of the bed. The IV had been taken out
previously, so she was fully mobile once again. "I
didn't notice that the gown detracted from you," he
told her wryly. "Beauty transcends such things."

Heat stung Abby's cheeks. She liked the officer's
dry sense of humor. "Our American men could learn
something from you," she said, placing her legs
across the bed, the deck cool beneath her bare feet.

It was time to leave, but Alec hesitated at the
hatch. "You must tell me more of what that means

while we eat our dinner later. I'll be in Dr. Ryback's office, waiting for you. Captain Stratman had your luggage brought over." He pointed to it sitting in the corner next to her bed. "Once you've showered and dressed, come join me."

Abby nodded and watched as the officer pulled the hatch partially closed to give her privacy. For a moment, she sat on the bed, just getting used to the ship's rolling movement. The deck tilted slightly one way, and then the other. The *Argonaut,* because of its small size, had been like a small cork on the Bering Sea, so the destroyer was infinitely more stable in comparison. Still, the dizziness came and went, and she didn't want to risk further injury by being too spontaneous about sliding off the bed too soon.

An hour later, she appeared at the entrance to Dr. Ryback's office. Alec immediately stood up from behind the desk, which, like all the furniture, was bolted to the deck so it couldn't be tossed around. When she stepped hesitantly across the hatch, Alec's eyes widened in appreciation. Although Abby's hair was still damp, it hung in shining copper curls about her shoulders. She wore a pair of decidedly old blue jeans that lovingly outlined her long legs. The sweatshirt had the endangered minke whale emblazoned on it.

"Come," Alec invited, "sit down. Our steward just brought us these dinner trays."

Abby chose a metal chair near the desk. "I'm so starved I could eat sushi!"

Alec brought the tray over to her. Abby's long fingers curved delicately around the edges of the tray. There was little about her, Alec decided, that wasn't beautiful or graceful. "Sushi? What is that?" He went back to his seat behind the desk and took the cover off his tray.

"Raw fish. Everyone eats it over in Japan, and it's all the rage in the States now." Abby stared down at the tray. There were two thick, greasy lengths of sausage, a slice of black bread, some boiled cabbage and a thin, watery soup with more cabbage floating in it.

Alec watched Abby's mobile features. Her fine, thin eyebrows drew into a worried line as she studied the contents on her tray. "And you prefer raw food to cooked food?" he wondered aloud. Was that why she was looking disappointed?

"Uhhh...no, as a matter of fact, I can't stand sushi. My friend Susan Stone, who lives across the hall from me with her daughter, loves it. We went to her boss's home a month ago for a dinner party." Abby lifted her head and managed a weak smile. "I didn't realize it was a sushi party, and neither did Susan."

"You couldn't eat it?"

She shivered. "Ugh! No way."

Alec waited for her to take the first bite. That was proper dinner etiquette, to allow the lady to begin eating first. He was starving, so he silently wished that Abby would begin eating her meal. However, he was too polite, too much of a gentleman, to suggest such a thing to her. "And so, did you starve that night?"

With a roll of her eyes, Abby laughed. "I grabbed Susan and we sneaked into the kitchen. The caterer made me a peanut butter sandwich instead. Susan's a wonderful friend," Abby said with feeling. "She puts up with me and my many eccentricities."

Patience was something Alec had by heritage. He watched as Abby's hands moved gracefully as she talked. She was never still. "Then," he said tactfully, "this meal should appeal to you. Nothing is raw or uncooked." With more pride, he added, "The food you are about to eat is served only to the officers on board. Meat is a very rare commodity for us, and the steward has given you a double portion. Please, eat."

Distressed, Abby took her spoon and tried the thin soup. It was bland, with no hint of seasoning, just a slight taste of cabbage flavor to the broth. She saw the officer watching her, almost hawklike. "It's good. Really good," she lied.

Unsure, Alec picked up his silverware and began to eat methodically. "While you were showering, I talked to First Captain Denisov, the commander of our destroyer. The seas are calming down, and he anticipates we'll reach Kodiak in five days."

"Good," Abby said, finishing off the small bowl of soup. She took her fork and moved it through the heaping strands of cut and boiled cabbage. It was dripping in grease, and she hesitated.

"Is there something wrong with the food?"

Abby chewed on her lower lip and chanced a look at the officer. "I—well, it's awfully greasy. You know—cholesterol."

"I beg your pardon?"

She laid the limp cabbage back on the tray and put the fork aside. "In America, half the deaths each year are due to heart attacks because we eat too much meat, and too many other foods with high cholesterol in them. The fat clogs your arteries and gives you heart problems." She gave a delicate shrug and her voice became apologetic. "I'm sorry, I just can't eat the cabbage or sausage, Alec. It's too greasy. And besides that, I'm a strict vegetarian."

Frowning, he tried to table his hurt over her decision not to eat the costly and rare meat. "A vegetarian?"

"Yes. I don't eat any kind of meat, including seafood. I eat lots of other things, though," Abby said quickly, seeing that his features mirrored injury. "Rice, bread, any kind of fruits, vegetables, lots of salads, nuts and things like that." She watched as he grew more distressed. "I'm sorry. I imagine it's tough to keep lots of fresh fruits and vegetables on board. You've done your best to feed me. It's my problem."

"No, you need to eat something."

"The soup and bread are fine. Really." With a slight smile, Abby added, "Did you know half the people in my country are overweight?"

Alec motioned to her. "That may be so, but you're too thin." He was confused by her explanation, thinking Americans had strange ideas about food and health customs.

Abby looked down at herself. "I know. Susan gets on me about that all the time. But I'm so busy with SOWF matters that I'm constantly traveling. And when I travel, I don't eat much."

Getting up, Alec brought his bowl of soup over to her, plus a thick slice of black bread. "I won't be responsible for you losing any more weight, then. Here, eat these. The bread is rich and nutritious. I'll order more if you like."

Touched, Abby took his offering without protest. Alec could have rightfully acted rebuffed by her eccentric eating habits, but he didn't. She watched as he ordered her another large bowl of soup and four more slices of the black bread. Not wanting to appear more ungrateful, she began to eat in earnest, even though the soup was little more than water. If Alec considered the food he ate as an officer good, what on earth did the crew eat?

After the meal, Abby was pleasantly full. The trays were taken away by a teenage steward with sandy hair. He tried to glance at her inconspicuously, without appearing rude about his curiosity. When he left, Alec grinned.

"You know you are a celebrity on the ship, don't you?"

"No."

"There are no women on board, and so when the crew found out we had rescued a red-haired American woman, the rumors began to fly. This young steward will go back to his quarters after his watch and tell everyone how he actually saw you, that you aren't a rumor at all, but very much alive and beautiful."

"I feel very pampered and cared for, Alec. Thanks to you."

He smiled and barely tipped his head in her direction. "So, let me show you to your quarters. Captain Stratman has asked that when you feel like it, he'd like to talk to you on the radio. I can take you up to the bridge after we deliver your luggage to your quarters."

With food in her stomach, Abby felt her returning strength. "I'd like that."

By the time they arrived on the bridge, dusk had fallen across the Bering Sea. Abby felt the intense stares of the crew, who tried to look at her discreetly. In America, they'd gape. First Captain Denisov was a barrellike man, his hair steel gray just like his eyes. His skin was ruddy, and his smile genuinely filled with welcome.

"Rostov, I see you've brought our guest to me." He stretched out his hand in Abby's direction. "Glad to see you alive and well, Dr. Fielding."

Denisov's handshake was powerful and Abby quickly released his grip. She gave the skipper her thanks not only for the rescue, but for the care afterward.

"It's nothing." Denisov gestured to the rear of the bridge. "Take a look. There is the *Argonaut,* who is in surprisingly good shape after the collision."

Abby was glad that Alec remained at her side. The destroyer had several spotlights focused on the *Argonaut* from its array of radar, radio antennas and other equipment positioned above the bridge. The small trawler was being expertly towed from the stern of the destroyer. Denisov ordered the radioman to make contact with Captain Stratman for her.

Alec led Abby to the console so that she could talk to the American skipper. He showed her how to operate the microphone and then handed it to her.

"Abby!" Stratman boomed over the radio, "Are you all right, girl?"

She laughed and held the microphone close to her lips while looking out the thick window toward the *Argonaut.* "I'm fine, John. Just fine."

"Thank all the saints. Girl, I thought for sure you were goin' down for the count."

Abby glanced up at Alec, who stood relaxed and yet alert nearby. "I had a very brave navigation officer by the name of Second Captain Alec Rostov save my life, John."

"Yeah, I didn't see your rescue. I had my hands full just getting the *Argonaut* out of the way of that Japanese catcher. Hey! Things are cookin', gal."

"Oh?"

"Yeah. Did you know that the Soviet helicopter that rescued you photographed the whole event? And Brad got it on video, too. Captain Denisov has agreed to lend us a copy of their film and a copy of a follow-up article that's being prepared by a reporter from Izvestia. How about that? Brad is already on the radio with Anchorage about what happened. Some SOWF representative, a Tony Cummings, is flying out to Kodiak to pick up the film and article and take them back to Anchorage for release to the press. He's going to take Brad's video of the collision, too. Tony's hoping that the national news networks will carry the story. Ain't that great? We might get national airtime!"

"Oh, John, that's wonderful! Wonderful!" Abby glanced up at Alec. His features were shadowed and thoughtful, his eyes never leaving her face. It sent her heart pounding suddenly in her chest. Distracted, Abby asked, "John, what are you doing about the Japanese ship? Have you filed a protest yet? Did they stop trying to follow the pods of humpback whales?"

"Whoa! One question at a time. No, girl, I'm afraid they haven't stopped hunting the whales. Yes, I've filed a protest, but you know how that goes. The U.S. hasn't been enforcing the Pelly and Magnuson

Amendments that're supposed to slap the hands of
these countries illegally hunting the endangered
whales. So you know my protest will fall on deaf ears
in Washington. Listen, don't worry about all these
details. You nearly died out there this morning. Just
get well. I've already got repairs underway here.
We'll patch up the *Argonaut* in Kodiak and be ready
to come back out here and give 'em hell again.''

Her fingers tightened painfully around the microphone. ''John, we've got to stop them! I don't care
what the cost.''

''The cost was almost your life today, Abby,'' he
warned seriously. ''Next time, we might not be so
lucky.''

''Next time, we'll do the same thing,'' Abby whispered, her voice vibrating with anger. ''Those whales
have no way to protect themselves from a harpoon.
We're all that stands between them and death. No,
John, we'll be going back out as soon as repairs are
made to your ship.''

''Okay, girl, you always did get your way when
you wanted it.'' He laughed. ''But stand by for action. If Tony can get us national news coverage, it
ought to really turn up the heat internationally on the
Japanese, Icelandic and Norwegian whalers who are
defying the ban on endangered whales. Good work,
girl. Gotta sign off for now. I'll talk to you tomorrow morning, eh?''

"Okay, John. Thanks...thanks for everything. It took a lot of courage to stare down the mouth of that catcher this morning."

With a chuckle, Stratman said, "Now I know how Jonah felt just before the whale swallowed him," then he signed off.

Abby handed the microphone back to Alec and thanked him.

Denisov came over. "I think you should know, Dr. Fielding, that we've been communicating with your U.S. Coast Guard stationed at Kodiak." He smiled slightly at Alec and continued. "Apparently your brave encounter with the Japanese whaler is making waves of its own with the press from around the world. The Coast Guard informed us just before you came up to the bridge that they are giving us permission to enter Kodiak with the *Argonaut*. But there is one more surprise. The international press awaits both of you in Anchorage."

Abby glanced up at Alec, who was scowling. "What does that mean, Captain Denisov?" she asked.

"A very large press conference is being prepared for you once we anchor in Kodiak." The stern planes of Denisov's face became more serious. "Captain Rostov, you have just been ordered by fleet headquarters to act as liaison officer to Dr. Fielding for the coming two weeks. When we arrive in Kodiak, both of you will be picked up by Coast Guard helicopter and flown directly to the Hotel Captain Cook in Anchorage for the press conference. The video and the film will be shown, and both of you will answer the press's questions.''

Stunned by the turn of events, Alec cleared his throat. ''Sir, I'm not really a public-affairs officer—''

''Moscow has faith in your ability to tell the story as it happened,'' Denisov replied. ''When you reach Anchorage, you are to escort Dr. Fielding to the various press and television stations. A Coast Guard officer will also be your liaison. Congratulations. *Glasnost* at its finest will be seen in action by the entire world.''

Alec nodded, stunned by the news. ''Thank you, Captain.'' He saw Abby smile, her eyes shining with such life that the assignment seemed insignificant compared to the fact he'd be with her for two weeks. The thought was tantalizing. Provocative.

''Wonderful!'' Abby added, giving both men a winning smile. ''It will give me a chance to show you a little of America, Alec.''

Denisov's eyebrows rose, no doubt over Abby's informalities. Hiding his nervousness, Alec smiled. ''With *glasnost* a priority, Dr. Fielding, I'll be happy as a representative of the U.S.S.R. naval service to be shown your country and way of life.''

''Brother, are you in for a treat,'' Abby teased warmly.

Alec could see dark shadows beginning to form beneath Abby's glorious blue eyes. He gently cupped her elbow. "I think, Doctor, that you are getting very tired. Let me take you to your quarters. Tomorrow will be a busy day, I'm sure."

His touch was light but firm. Abby was surprised that he could tell she was getting tired. The trauma from nearly drowning this morning had caught up with her. She told Captain Denisov goodbye, then followed Alec off the bridge and onto one of the lower decks of the destroyer.

"Are you always a mind reader?" she asked as they walked single file down a narrow passageway deep in the heart of the rolling ship.

"I think," Alec told her seriously, stopping at a hatchway and opening it for her, "that any good officer tries to stay in touch with his crew's moods and needs. It is his duty." He gazed down at her in the shadowy light, her red hair curlier now since it had dried. He had a wild, unexpected urge to thrust his fingers through that mass and explore its silken texture. "I merely applied my powers of observation."

Abby stepped across the hatch and into her very small quarters. Two of the officers had given over to her their cramped living area, which consisted of two thin bunks, one above the other. "I think, Captain Rostov, that there's much more to you than what you show the rest of the world."

His lips lifted slightly. "You have the same perceptiveness as I do, Abby."

"Does it bother you?"

He shrugged his broad shoulders. "If you were another officer on board the ship, it might. But you're a woman and an American, so I have little to fear about what you might see in me."

Abby stood there for a long moment, digesting the seriousness of his comment to her, his sable-colored eyes smoldering with an intensity that made her deliciously aware that she was a woman. "We'll have to talk more," she whispered. "Good night, Alec. And again, thanks for everything." Impulsively, she threw her arms around his neck and gave him a quick hug. Releasing him, she stepped back and smiled shyly. "That was my western upbringing coming out."

His body tingled where she had lightly pressed herself against him. Shocked by her impulsiveness, Alec nodded and came to attention. "It was my pleasure, Abby," he said with a slight bow. "I think I'm beginning to like your western customs more and more."

Chapter Three

"What do you think of all this excitement and press interest that's building, Rostov?" Dr. Ryback asked Alec at mess the next morning. Two stewards, dressed in white jackets and slacks, served the ten officers in the small rectangular room.

Alec was careful with his words. "I feel it's a useful opportunity for us to expand awareness of *glasnost* to the world, Doctor." Every ship had its KGB agents, the eyes and ears of the clandestine spy organization. Alec had no desire to be quoted saying the wrong thing.

Denisov chuckled, hungrily digging into a mound of powdered scrambled eggs and fried potatoes. "You must have very good connections in Moscow, Rostov. I envy you the chance to see what America is really like."

"We'll soon find out if they are gangsters and cowboys," Alec agreed. The perception of Americans was just that and little more. He wasn't about to admit the intensity of his curiosity about going ashore with Abby and learning about her way of life. Over the years, in order to maintain his facility with English, he read any book on America whenever possible. Alec had done some checking last night on the bridge when it was his turn for watch. The messages from Moscow had been signed by Misha Surin, his friend at the Kremlin, and countersigned by the admiral of the Soviet pacific fleet. Obviously, the hierarchy in Moscow thought his rescue of Abby was something to be paraded in front of the world press.

Chuckling, Denisov waved his fork in Alec's direction. "Make us all proud, Rostov. Who knows? If you do well with the American press, we may all receive a *glasnost* medal for helping continue to warm the relations between our two countries. Not a bad reward, eh?"

One of the stewards opened the hatch entrance from the passageway and Abby Fielding entered. Immediately, all ten officers leapt to their feet. Alec suppressed a smile as Abby stood there, shock written across her still-sleepy features. Today she had taken her thick hair and braided it in a decidedly feminine style down the back of her head. The wispy bangs barely grazed her eyebrows, and playful tendrils touched her temples. She looked excruciatingly beautiful in his eyes in a simple wardrobe of jeans and a long-sleeved white blouse. A dark blue sweater was hung across her back and shoulders, the arms crossed in a casual fashion across her breasts. The image was fetching. Refreshing.

"Good morning," Alec said in greeting, leaving his chair and going over to her. "You are the guest of honor. I'll seat you next to Captain Denisov."

Flushing over such formality, Abby smiled and nodded. If the truth be known, she'd much rather have sat beside Alec, but she realized it would not have been prudent. "Good morning," she murmured huskily to all the serious-faced officers. Denisov looked delighted by her presence. When Alec offered her the seat and she sat down, the other naval officers returned to their chairs.

"You are like a rare spring rose aboard our humble naval vessel," Denisov told her in thick, heavy English. He waved the steward over and ordered him to serve her coffee and then had her plate heaped with eggs, potatoes and two portions of sausage.

"Thank you, Captain Denisov." Abby picked up the white ceramic mug filled with steaming hot coffee, needing the caffeine badly. Learning that she had to taste all Soviet food carefully, Abby took a small sip of the strong liquid. As much as she wanted to wrinkle her nose, Abby suppressed the desire. Denisov was watching her every move, wanting to be assured that his efforts pleased her. She forced a smile. "Your coffee is like the stuff I drink on the *Argonaut*—strong and rich." The "rich" was a white lie, but Denisov's face grew flushed with pleasure.

"Excellent! At least we share one thing in common, eh? Both American and Soviet coffee is good!

We purposely make our coffee strong to keep us hearty."

Abby knew she wasn't a diplomat and gracefully refrained from saying anything more, pretending instead to eat. The eggs, of course, were out of the question. The potatoes had been fried and lay in grease, like shining silver dollars on the white ceramic plate edged with red trim. The sausages stared at her, and she couldn't bear looking at them one moment longer. Discreetly, Abby played with the potatoes with her fork.

"Why not get Dr. Fielding some bread?" Alec suggested to one of the two young stewards.

Abby flashed Alec a grateful look she hoped he would interpret as a silent thank-you. She found his sable eyes twinkling knowingly, and she suddenly realized how much she missed Alec's teasing and lighthearted banter in comparison to the rest of the solemn sailors and officer on board the *Udaloy*. From them there was never a smile, a joke or a laugh, just unrelenting formality. Alec was different, Abby had decided this morning as she was being escorted to mess by the chief from the dispensary.

"You know," Denisov said, "at sea we sometimes don't get news from home as often as we'd like. Tell me, what is happening in your country right now? What is newsworthy?"

Abby blotted her lips with the white linen napkin and searched her memory. "Well, I've been out to sea for a week, Captain, so what I remember will probably be old news.''

He shrugged dramatically. ''We rarely get news from America at all, so perhaps you will indulge us with this 'old' news?''

She smiled. ''Sure. Our Supreme Court just approved a hiring preference for women and minorities.''

''Why is that important?''

''Because women in America are considered second-class citizens, Captain. We're fighting for equality in all phases of our life. And that means that employers can no longer discriminate and hire a man for a job that a woman can do as well.''

''Interesting,'' Denisov murmured. ''You know, in the Soviet Union, our women are just as strong and work right alongside our men.''

Abby smiled. ''No, I didn't know.''

''So what is this I hear about you not only having an actor for a president, but now a mayor, as well?''

Deciding that Denisov was rather well-informed whether he was at sea or not, Abby grinned. ''Clint Eastwood, an actor from Hollywood, was just voted in as mayor of Carmel-by-the-Sea.''

''Is your country run only by actors?''

''Sometimes,'' Abby said seriously, ''I think so. But, that's a personal opinion. President Reagan is very popular with a lot of people.''

''Yet, you don't care for him?''

"I don't care for some of his politics," Abby stressed. "In our country, we're allowed to dissent and voice our own opinion, whether it's popular or not."

Denisov's bushy gray brows rose, but he said nothing. "Your brush with the Japanese whaler is only the tip of the iceberg, it seems."

"Oh?"

"Hasn't your president just blocked three-million-dollars worth of Japanese merchandise from coming into your country in retaliation for Japan not honoring a trade agreement regarding semiconductors?"

Abby gave the captain a blank look, rummaged through her memory and then said, "Yes, he did just impose that embargo."

"What of sports?"

"I don't know very much about sports, Captain."

"Boxing? Is there anything going on? It is my favorite sport."

"I think I recall Sugar Ray Leonard beating Marvin Hagler for the middleweight championship of the world."

Grinning, Denisov said, "Good! Sports are the lifeblood of men."

Silently, Abby agreed. She hated football and any other sport. To her, it was a waste of time to be glued to the television set for an entire weekend, watching one sporting event after another. "You and every man in America agree upon that," she muttered.

"What other bits of news do you recall?"

Abby sighed inwardly. Were the next four days at breakfast going to consist of Denisov questioning her at length? She wondered if she should be speaking about anything at all, but then decided that she knew so little of matters related to national security that it wouldn't hurt to entertain the cagey captain.

"Let's see . . . one of our huge oil companies, Texaco, just filed for bankruptcy. That's been a real shock to the nation. My friend Susan is a stock broker, and she says it's going to send a scare through the financial district of Wall Street."

With a nod, Denisov pushed aside his plate. Immediately, one of the stewards came and picked it up. "I heard that one of your air force Centaur rockets blew up less than a minute after takeoff from Cape Canaveral." He studied her intently. "A year ago, you lost the *Challenger* in that unfortunate mishap. I understand your country is having a hard time placing satellites into orbit without the space shuttle. This Centaur was supposed to have been struck by lightning, veered off course and had to be destroyed. Is this true?"

Squirming, Abby shrugged. "Got me on that one, Captain. Things like sports, military or entertainment items don't interest me. I sort of ignore them in favor of politics, which is an area that interests me greatly. Sorry, I don't know anything about the rocket exploding.'' She was lying, of course, but didn't care. Looking down at Alec, she saw him frowning.

Abby tried to relax and adjust to the situation. Denisov was going to pump her, and she was simply going to evade and play dumb when she felt it necessary. In one way, Abby wanted the next four days to pass quickly. But on a personal level, she wanted them to stretch out and slow down. She suddenly wanted the time to know one Alec Rostov better.

ON THE FIFTH MORNING ABOARD the *Udaloy,* Abby spent breakfast with the officers, as usual. Denisov was in a good mood, smiling often and laughing easily. In the past week Abby found ways to manipulate the conversations with the curious captain. She talked about several books she'd brought aboard the *Argonaut* to read at night when their whale-watch duties were done.

Denisov found *Destiny* by Sally Beauman interesting, although he wasn't much of a reader of women's fiction. The entire table became animated and engrossed when she discussed *Texasville* by Larry McMurty, because it was about the Old West, and she discovered the Soviets' keen curiosity with anything having to do with that time in her nation's history. Abby decided not to discuss *State Scarlet* by David Aaron with them because it was a political hot potato sprinkled liberally with intrigue and national-defense information.

Another morning, Abby talked about the Broadway plays in New York City, and a lively discussion ensued as to whether the Bolshoi could compare. Having just seen *Blythe Spirit* by Noël Coward, Abby shared the plot of the play with them. She discovered the Soviets had a deep and loyal tie to the arts, and breakfast soon became a place to share such information. When she told them she'd seen the ballet *Sleeping Beauty* at New York's Metropolitan Opera House, they excitedly told her about the Bolshoi.

Perhaps the most political she got was in telling them about *The Jaguar Smiles* by Salman Rushdie, a book that was written about the Sandinista government in Nicaragua. When it got too political, Abby gracefully evaded the topic and deftly turned the conversation to Vincent Van Gogh's painting *Sunflowers,* which sold recently for 39.9 million dollars. The officers at the table simply couldn't comprehend such money being spent on one painting, despite their love of the arts.

Denisov smiled. "While you slept this morning, Tony Cummings landed on our helo pad and took the film and official report of your rescue, and then left," Denisov told her. "He said to tell you hello and to give you this." He produced a thick manila envelope. "It is your information for the forthcoming press conference in Anchorage. I would hope that you would share its contents with Captain Rostov in order to help him prepare for the reporters' questions."

"Of course," Abby murmured. She placed the heavy envelope across her lap, having the distinct feeling that Denisov would have preferred her to open it and share the contents in front of him, but she resisted. "Would it be possible for Captain Rostov to go over the information with me after breakfast?"

Beaming, Denisov nodded. "Excellent idea, Dr. Fielding. Excellent idea."

IN ANOTHER STAFF ROOM AFTER the meal, Alec sat down with Abby. The coast of Kodiak Island was clearly in sight now, and by tomorrow morning, the *Udaloy* would arrive at the twelve-mile limit of U.S. coastal waters. It was Abby's understanding that a Coast Guard helicopter would land on the *Udaloy*, pick up her and Alec, and fly them directly to Anchorage for the press conference at noon.

Although the hatch to the small room was shut and no sound could be heard, Alec didn't trust the room not to be bugged. Taking out a pen and paper from the breast pocket of his dark blue uniform blouse, he scribbled a note and placed it in front of Abby.

This room may be bugged. Watch what you say. If there are sensitive things that need to be said,

I suggest a walk on deck where there are no prying ears, just prying eyes.

Frowning, Abby nodded. She watched as Alec took the note and placed it in a pocket. She quickly shook out the contents of Tony's envelope on the table before them.

"Oh, look!" Abby exclaimed, pleased. There was a color photo taken from the video Brad had shot of the Japanese ship bearing down on the *Argonaut.* The video had been flown to Kodiak Island by the long range Helix yesterday. The effort had been worth it. "Brad got some great shots!" she whispered excitedly, looking through the ten photos. "This is awesome. Simply awesome!"

"'Awesome'?"

Looking up, Abby realized the word confounded Alec. "It's a slang phrase we use in America. We seem to go through certain words in our culture every decade. In the sixties, it was *groovy* and *far out.* Today it's *awesome.* Do you go through phrases like that in Russia?"

He shook his head. "No."

Abby wanted to say that so far, all the men she'd met from the Soviet Union had very little to say— ever. She wondered why. Was it the brooding tenor of Communism that had forced them to all behave in such a low-key manner? Returning her attention to the articles, Abby noticed several newspaper clippings that Tony had copied for her. "Take a look at these, Alec." She rapidly scanned several articles.

"You're a hero in every major newspaper in the U.S.! Just look at these!"

For the next half hour, Alec poured over the mound of newspaper articles. In amazement, he glanced at Abby. "This is simply incredible."

She grinned happily. "If it will get my whales this kind of attention, I'd do it all over again."

Cocking his head, Alec studied her. The room was stuffy. "Would you like some fresh air?"

Abby immediately caught his inference. "I'd love some. I need my daily exercise anyway." Every day they took a stroll out on the deck of the destroyer, if the weather cooperated. Alec shrugged into his dark blue parka and settled the trooper cap of the same color on his head. Abby quickly retrieved her cranberry-colored wool jacket and white scarf.

Out on the deck of the *Udaloy,* the morning sun was shining brightly across the gray-green Bering Sea. The weather had held up surprisingly well for the entire week, but the sea was confused this morning, so Alec kept a hold on Abby's elbow as he guided her out onto the helicopter landing pad. It was the best place to talk privately.

The wind had a decided bite to it, and Abby brought the collar up to protect her neck. She scrunched her hands deep into her pockets. From the fantail she could easily see the *Argonaut* in tow, and her three friends up on the small glass-enclosed bridge. Waving energetically to them, Abby saw them all return her greeting. It was impossible to visit them while the trawler was in tow, so she had to be content with waving to them.

"Your friends miss you," Alec observed as they came to a halt and stood together on the center of the landing pad area.

"I miss them. John and I have done a lot of whale protecting from that old salmon trawler of his over the last three years. The SOWF funds pay for his gas, but John volunteers his time." She looked up at Alec's square-jawed face, those dark brown eyes upon her. It sent a ribbon of warmth through Abby. She liked the gentle light she saw in Alec's thoughtful gaze.

"Why did you write that note to me?"

He shifted and stood close to Abby, the destroyer constantly rolling from side to side or pitching up and down. Although the waves were only three to four feet in height, the destroyer could hit waves going in a different direction or a rogue wave many times higher, and Abby might lose her balance and fall. "Because most of the rooms are bugged."

"Oh...."

With a grimace, Alec said, "We have KGB agents aboard and no one knows who they are. We must watch what we say at all times, I think, when it comes to discussing the forthcoming press conference."

She grinned. "Good thing I didn't say anything about those greasy sausages or potatoes I got three mornings in a row, then."

Alec's laugh was full and resonant. "I'm glad you didn't. Captain Denisov wanted everything perfect for you. He had finally realized you're a vegetarian and you won't eat the meat, no matter how prized it is to us. The Captain has taken it in good stride, though. I'm glad our cooks found some rice for you, otherwise you might have starved to death on cabbage soup and black bread." His smile deepened as he absorbed Abby's flushed features into his heart. She was so alive, so incredibly spontaneous compared to the women of the Soviet Union. "In all truth, most of us are forced into being vegetarians because there is so little meat available in our country."

"You make vegetarianism sound like a bread-and-water prison sentence," Abby said with a laugh, "and it isn't. Actually, I've enjoyed your black bread, just as I've enjoyed being with the crew and having our spirited talks at the breakfast table. But you've been evading me all week," she teased him. "I know so little about you personally, Alec. From what Tony's letter said, we'll be spending a week together in Anchorage. Couldn't you tell me a little bit more about yourself?"

Caught up in her enthusiasm, he nodded. "I didn't mean not to talk about myself, but I think Soviets remain like a closed book because of their fear of the KGB network of spies. I'll try, over the next day, to give you more personal vignettes about myself." He frowned. "I'm looking forward to the experience, but I hope my English is good enough so that I don't embarrass us with your press."

"Your English is flawless. In fact, far better than mine." She turned and faced him, the salt air invigorating, the wind whipping around them. "So, tell me about yourself. Everything!"

The destroyer pitched, and Alec automatically reached out, his fingers wrapping around her arm. Abby moved closer to him, and he felt a powerful need to protect her, even though he knew she was fully capable of taking care of herself. Although, Alec reminded himself, Abby had a decided reckless streak when it came to protecting her whales.

"I was born and raised in Moscow thirty years ago. My parents are both medical doctors who work in a hospital in the same city. My mother, Darya Rostov, is a pediatrician. My father, Konstantin Rostov, is a brilliant cardiac surgeon. When I entered the university, I majored in mathematics with a minor in communications. I also took four years of English because of my minor, and it has proven a good thing. It has given me assignments where an English-speaking officer has been needed." He looked down at her rapt features. "I knew I had to spend time in the military, so I selected the navy. After three years, I had fallen in love with the ocean, so I've chosen to remain as a navigation officer. I just recently left the Baltic Sea Command and was transferred here to the Bering area."

"Any brothers or sisters?"

He shook his head.

"I don't have any, either."

"We're alike in several ways. You are a marine biologist who loves the sea, and we are the only children in a marriage."

"I think that's why I'm so bullheaded about what I do," Abby said with a slight smile. "My father is a cetacean scientist who works at Scripps Oceanographic Institute near San Diego. My mother has a degree in biology, but she's very active in women's-rights issues. She's a lobbyist, and her main concerns are for single, divorced mothers raising a family, adequate day-care for their children and equal-rights issues."

"Lobbyist?"

"That's a person whose job it is to persuade our senators and congressman to vote in favor of the issues for which the lobbyist advocates," Abby explained.

"Are you a lobbyist, then, for whale issues?"

"No, although environmental organizations use my knowledge and my name when they go before Congress to push for enforcement of the Pelly and Magnuson Amendments. Sometimes I'm called to testify before a House or Senate hearing regarding endangered whale species such as the humpback and minke whales." Her eyebrows lowered. "And I've got my detractors on the Hill. Dr. Monica Turner, an assistant from the State Department, hates me on sight. She's probably rolling her eyes over all the press attention your rescue of me has gotten. Actually, it's probably jealousy more than anything. Dr. Turner has the ear of President Reagan, and she's antiwhale. She and I have locked horns before. Her negative whale stance is well-known, and Reaganomics doesn't exactly favor protecting anything environmental, believe me," Abby said grimly. "So, it's always an uphill battle with Congress to persuade them how real the danger is, not only to certain whale species but to dolphins."

"Well," Alec said in a hopeful tone, "you will get your chance to see the American public on your side of this issue when we get to Anchorage."

"For being a Soviet, you very astutely see the problems and possible answers," Abby told him, impressed with his intelligent assessment.

With a chuckle, Alec said, "I don't think it has anything to do with the country in which one is born, but rather, a sensitivity and awareness that politics is a part of the fabric of everyone's life—whether we like it or not."

Suddenly, Abby was thrilled as never before at the prospect of having Alec at her side during the week in Anchorage. "You do know I live in Anchorage part-time, don't you?"

"No, I didn't."

"When the whales come up from Baja, Mexico, every spring, I live in Alaska and try to protect them while they feed in the Bering and Chuckhi seas. From November through January, I live in my other apartment near Washington, D.C., where I work with SOWF lobbyists and do a lot of political work on behalf of the whales and dolphins. Then, in late January through April, I'm down in the Baja, Mexico area doing research on humpbacks at their breeding and calving ground off the Rivillagigedo Islands, or on the gray whales off the lagoons of Baja. Next January, I'll be working with several distinguished marine biologists from other worldwide scientific organizations in the San Ignacio Lagoon off Baja, filming gray whales giving birth. We'll all be staying on the science ship *Seafarer*."

"You're a very busy person," he said, "but I like your commitment. You don't just give words to what you care about, you actually go out there and do something about it."

Abby grinned. "The story of my life, Alec. I'm always up to my red hair in trouble of some sort because of my whales."

He laughed. "That doesn't surprise me. I must see your apartment in Anchorage, though, because I want to compare it to our way of life in the Soviet Union."

"Not only will you see it," she promised him seriously, "I intend to make you some home-cooked meals. Real American food. Well, actually, vegetarian or meat fare, but I promise, it will be good."

Alec watched the hazy-blue land mass that was drawing closer and closer. It was Kodiak Island, the mountainous terrain covered with a rich cloak of verdant forest. His heart picked up in beat, not because of the beauty of what he saw, but because Abby, who was childlike in her enthusiasm, touched him as no other woman ever had. He smiled down at her.

"Home-cooked food is something I've had too little of," he told her fervently.

"Well," she added with a groan, "I'll have to take you to McDonald's, too. I want you to get a real slice of American life."

"McDonald's?"

"Yes, a very American fast-food chain of restaurants. You'll love it since you're an avid meat eater."

"I'm sure I will, but I still want to know more about your whale-saving activities."

With a laugh, Abby turned and faced him. "Don't worry! I'll probably bore you to death with information on them." In the morning sunlight she was able to see the ruddiness in Alec's cheeks, the wind whipping around them. The dark blue trooper cap he wore had a red-and-gold hammer-and-sickle insignia on the front. The rugged quality of his face had been shaped by the fierce and relentless ocean over a period of years. When the corners of his well-shaped mouth pulled upward, her heart pounded briefly in her breast, as if to underscore how handsome he was in her eyes.

"I have a friend in Moscow," Alec told her, "someone high up in the Kremlin. The Soviet Union has already agreed to the ban on killing whales, and

I feel my friend can be of help to us. How, I'm not sure, but if you'll get me the information on your whales, I'll make sure it's passed on to him.''

"Who knows," Abby said wistfully, "The Soviet Union might get more active as a result of this incident."

With a shrug of his shoulders, Alec said, "No one can any longer guess what the Kremlin will do. With General Secretary Gorbachev, the old way of life as we know it is rapidly changing."

"I hope he's a whale lover," Abby said fiercely under her breath. "We can use another powerful nation on our side."

With a laugh, Alec led her back toward the hatchway. It was freezing cold on deck and he realized that Abby was getting chilled by the way she was rubbing her hands together to keep them warm. "Come, let's share some hot coffee, warm up, then get back to work on our Anchorage adventure."

When the white H-65 Coast Guard helicopter with a red-orange stripe on its tail landed on the *Udaloy* to take them to Anchorage, Abby's excitement tripled. On board, she and Alec met their liaison officer, Lieutenant Tim Atkin. He had reddish hair cut military short and dancing brown eyes that told her of his intelligence. His smile, warm with welcome, won Abby over instantly. Privately, she'd been afraid that the Coast Guard might prove more of a deterrent than a friend. Tim's handshake was firm, and his boyish smile and the freckles across his nose and cheeks convinced Abby he was on their side.

Putting on the helmets Tim supplied them inside the aircraft gave Abby and Alec immediate communications with one another. After they slipped into the mandatory life vests, the Coast Guard helicopter lifted off the deck of the *Udaloy*. Abby waved out the window to Captain Denisov and his fellow officers below. She had made many new friends and was going to miss her table companions on board the destroyer.

Tim filled them in on the busy schedule ahead of them while the helicopter flew toward Anchorage. He also gave both of them a brief overview of his qualifications. At twenty-nine years old, he'd already been a skipper aboard an eighty-two foot Coast Guard cutter and had recently earned a master's degree in public administration from Harvard University. That meant he was not only savvy about the political process but was comfortable with the press. Tim knew how to manipulate the media in a positive way.

Abby watched as Tim focused his attention on Alec and told him what was expected from him in his week-long whirlwind tour of Anchorage. Both were in their respective uniforms, and Abby thought that history was being made with that handshake: two former enemies now working toward neutrality, if not friendship. There was clearly a respect between them when Alec discovered that the lieutenant had been a skipper of his own vessel. Although Atkin looked very young, he had the wisdom of someone twice his age.

"We've got a real tempest in a teapot," Tim told Abby wryly as they sat on one side of the helicopter in the nylon-webbed seats. "If you wanted press, you've got it." He smiled. "It's my job to get you to Hotel Captain Cook, where the official conference will take place." He looked up at Alec. "We've got a room for you in the hotel, Captain. Coast Guard personnel will be outside your door to stop the press from hounding you once the conference is over."

Abby reached out, gripping the officer's arm. "Why can't Alec stay at my apartment, Lieutenant? I have a guest bedroom. Wouldn't it be easier to guard both of us at the same address?"

Atkin nodded thoughtfully. "Great idea, Doctor. I'll radio my superiors about it, and if they approve, I'll put in a call to Captain Denisov and clear it with him. I don't see why they wouldn't approve the change in plans."

"Awesome."

Alec grinned for the first time that day. He wanted to shield Abby even though she was thoroughly capable of handling the press. In fact, she was eager to utilize the reporters to get the SOWF message out. He found her fierce belief in the whales a precious discovery. Until very recently, not many people in the Soviet Union would dare take on government policy the way Abby did. Even now, the Soviet people were

cautiously testing a new freedom Abby obviously
took for granted. There was something positive to
say for democracy, after all, Alec decided.

Abby turned to Alec. "Would you mind staying at
my place?"

"Not at all."

When Tim went to talk to the two pilots and radio
the request to Anchorage, Abby explained to Alec,
"Our Coast Guard isn't really a military service.
They're budgeted by the Department of Transportation. I've worked closely with them so many times,
especially on oil spills or chemical spills, that I'm
really glad they're orchestrating your stay. They have
top-notch, reliable people."

Alec watched Atkin speaking on the radio. There
was an energy around the Coast Guard officer that
impressed him immediately. He sensed Atkin was
one of those officers who very quietly, but smoothly,
got things done behind the scenes. "We've usually
had very good relations with the Coast Guard," he
told Abby.

Although she was dressed in a pair of jeans and a
sweater, Abby had brought along all the luggage
she'd taken to sea with her. Earlier, she had showed
Alec the outfit she would wear for the press conference. It was a pair of light tan wool slacks and an
accompanying blazer, an ivory blouse with ruffles
and a very old cameo given to her by her grandmother. Today, she informed him, she would have to
look official. Even her lovely hair, which Alec liked

to see loose and free about her shoulders, was tastefully arranged in a chignon at the nape of her neck. The earrings she wore were small gold dolphins. The pin on the lapel of her blazer was a gold whale. He smiled to himself. Abby wore her jewelry like a badge of courage for those mammals she had nearly given her life for. There was everything to admire about her.

"Okay, it's set," Tim Atkin told them sometime later as he rejoined them. "The Coast Guard has no objection, and I've got an okay from Captain Rostov." Tim pulled out several pages of paper from his attaché case and gave each of them a copy. "This is the itinerary for the week."

"Looks like a lot of activities," Abby said, surprised.

Tim smiled broadly. "Well, I had a little to do with it. The Coast Guard is proud to be a part of this *glasnost* opportunity. We thought Captain Rostov might like to see a little America, some tours, and to get a good look at the way we live."

"Wonderful!" Abby said, clapping her hands together.

"Have you penciled in time for me to sleep and eat, Lieutenant?" Alec asked with a smile.

Tim grinned broadly. "Yes, sir, I have." He pointed to Alec's copy of the itinerary. "After this first press conference, I'd like you to look over this schedule. If there's something on there you don't want to do, let me know. Or, if there's something that interests you that isn't on there, it can be added."

Alec nodded, fully impressed. "Thank you, Lieutenant."

Tim looked at them. "Well, are you ready to enter the fray after we land at Anchorage International Airport?"

Eagerly, Abby nodded. "You bet!"

Without thinking about his action, Alec gently laid his hand on Abby's arm. "I'm ready."

Her skin tingled where Alec had momentarily touched her. The sense of protection that he afforded her was new to Abby. He was always the officer and a gentleman, a far cry from the way a lot of men behaved toward women in the U.S. But then, Abby reminded herself, Alec was a Soviet, and his culture had far different moral codes and values. From what she had observed so far, Alec was very old-fashioned, and she liked that about him.

As she sat there in the confines of the helicopter, Abby wondered abruptly how Washington, D.C. would react to their press conference. She knew her mother, Vera, would be thrilled with the notoriety given the whales. On the other hand, she knew without doubt that Dr. Monica Turner from the State Department would probably be livid.

"I CAN'T BELIEVE THIS!" Monica Turner whispered. She was at her desk, watching the small television that sat in one corner of her massive office.

Her assistant secretary, Pat Monahan, had an unhappy look on her face as she stood near the set. "Every national news program has Abby Fielding's face plastered all over it!"

Pat shrugged delicately and switched off the set. "What worries me is the Soviet element. They sounded awfully pro whale and dolphin."

Angrily, Monica got up and moved to the venetian blinds behind her ornate maple desk. Out the window of her office, it was springtime. The cherry trees were blooming, and the lawns becoming green once more. "I think Fielding deliberately created that collision with the Japanese whaler just to get this kind of publicity. Damn those whale activists!" She clenched her fist behind her back. "They're like a plague, Pat. No, correct that—a damned virus. Just as bad as the AIDs virus, in my opinion."

"Well," Pat said with feeling, "don't let the press hear you say that. The SOWF would love to get a hold of you saying that about them."

"You're right. They'd milk it for all it's worth."

"Part of why they're so successful in getting publicity is because they know how to manipulate the media. I really worry if someone overhears your comments."

"Don't worry, I know how to manipulate the press, too," Monica muttered. "What makes me so angry is the fact that Fielding, on national television, has made disparaging remarks about President Reagan's policy regarding the environment. Doesn't

Fielding realize that whales aren't a priority anymore? She comes off like a self-righteous zealot. I'll bet she'd save a whale before she'd save a human being from death.''

Pat grimaced. ''We're going to have to work tonight with Hill personnel to issue some kind of statement.''

Monica turned, her eyes narrowing on her assistant. ''I'll write up some innocuous, generic response from the State Department that presents a united front between us and the president. Then you take it up the Hill and get it approved, Pat.''

''Of course.''

Grimly, Monica sat down and took some sheets of paper from her desk drawer. Her office was filled with mementos of the Reagan years. A favorite photo of her and the president sat on her desk, conspicuous, so that everyone would see it upon entering her mahogany-paneled office. Picking up her gold pen, she began to write.

''Fielding's not going to get away with this.''

Pat sighed. ''I don't know how we're going to stop them this time, Doctor. With that Soviet captain in tow, he's stealing the show with just his presence. *Glasnost* is in, and to tell you the truth, he's not bad-looking.''

''Speaks flawless English, too,'' Monica growled. ''Where'd they dig him up? Probably one of Gorbachev's minions they've been grooming for something like this.''

"While you're at it, don't you think an appropriate phone call to the Department of Transportation is in order, too? It appears that the Coast Guard approves of the views presented by Dr. Fielding. That isn't good for our image."

"Damned whale issue," Monica whispered, scribbling more rapidly on the paper. "I hate it! It's such a paltry problem in comparison to *real* problems like national-security issues! And Japan! God, but they're being stubborn about this semiconductor issue. But Fielding doesn't see that, does she? All she can see and hear is her stupid whales and dolphins!"

Sadly, Pat nodded her head. "Maybe this Captain Rostov will make a mistake and discredit himself with the American public. You know, *glasnost* is new, and the president is still leery of it."

"He ought to be. I am, too. Maybe Rostov is a mole. We'll see. Don't worry, Pat, I'm going to contact my friends at the FBI and have Rostov watched closely. Without his or the Coast Guard's knowledge, of course."

Pat smiled. "Wouldn't it be something if Abby Fielding was a deep-cover Russian spy?"

Chuckling, Monica shook her head. "Oh, if only that turned out to be true. Then I could discredit her and deflate this whole whale issue."

"Right now, she's looking like the good guy and the administration is the bad guy. All we can do is hope Fielding slips up and makes a fool of herself in some way."

Monica finished the statement with a flourish and handed it to her secretary to type up. "If she does, I'm going to be like a killer whale—just waiting to slit open her underbelly."

Chapter Four

"We're home," Abby announced wearily, stepping inside her Anchorage apartment. Alec followed her and halted in the middle of the living room to look around. Outside the door were two Coast Guard sentries, who would remain on twenty-four-hour duty until Alec's visit to the U.S. was at an end.

Glancing at her watch, Abby saw it was nearly 10:00 p.m. She quietly shut the pine door and watched Alec's inspection and his reactions. Realizing she'd never dreamed of seeing a Soviet in uniform in her home, the discovery left her shaken. Alec was a Russian who was, indeed, a friend, not an enemy.

"Well, what do you think?" she asked, walking past him into the kitchen.

Taking off his cap, Alec placed it beneath his left arm and moved around the living room. "It's spacious." He knew there was awe in his voice. "Very rich by Soviet standards. Someone who had power in the Kremlin or Politburo would have this kind of apartment."

Abby laughed and opened the fridge to retrieve a chilled bottle of wine. "Me, rich? Hardly. Marine biologists aren't rich. With my salary, some freelance writing and an occasional consulting fee, I make about twenty-seven thousand dollars a year. Here in the U.S. that's considered middle-class income, believe me." She brought two glasses down from the cupboard and glanced across the kitchen, which was separated from the living room by a breakfast bar.

The living room spoke of someone who respected the Earth, Alec thought. He leaned over to touch the cinnamon-colored velour sofa, and found the texture delightful. Potted plants hung from the ceiling and stood in huge ceramic pots. The hardwood floor was a gold-and-reddish-colored cedar, graced with a large hand-woven Navaho rug at its center. The coffee table was fashioned from pine, and a hand-carved mahogany whale was the centerpiece. The overstuffed chairs were a tan and a brick color respectively. The room gave off a sense of earthy warmth.

When Abby handed him a fluted glass of rose-colored wine, Alec smiled. "Thank you," he murmured.

"Sit down," Abby urged. "Take off your jacket, loosen your tie and kick off your shoes. You've got to be dead on your feet." She sat in one of the overstuffed chairs, dangling her long legs over one arm, and kicked off her sensible brown shoes.

Grinning, Alec took a sip of the wine and watched Abby. She was tired, as evidenced by the shadows beneath her glorious blue eyes. But she looked utterly wanton with her hair released from the pins that had held it captive all day.

She smiled at him. He looked so stiff and formal. "Come on! Relax, Alec. There's no camera around to take your photo now."

She was right. He put down the flute and tried to get comfortable. "I want you to know, this is the first time I've done this."

"What?" The wine, a blush variety from California, tasted heavenly to Abby after the long, grueling day. It had been a day filled with victories, though, not defeats. She felt high on adrenaline from all the media attention, not for herself, but for her whales and dolphins. They'd finally got the attention they deserved.

Alec shrugged out of his uniform jacket and laid it across the back of the couch. Off came his tie, and he opened the button of his shirt at his throat. "Getting out of uniform like this is against regulations. I either wear it or don't wear it. If Captain Denisov could see me," Alec said as he sat down to untie his shining black shoes, "he'd probably write me up for being out of uniform and a disgrace to the Soviet navy."

Giggling, Abby shook her head and threaded her fingers through her hair to loosen up the abundant mass. What she needed to do was brush it. She hated pinning it up in a chignon, but realized she had had to look professional today for the world's cameras. "I won't tell." With his light blue long-sleeved shirt opened at the throat, Alec looked like a businessman now, and not a naval officer. The only light on in the living room was a huge hanging stained-glass lamp, a pattern of red roses and green leaves on a pale pink background. It cast colorful light about, and the shadows accentuated Alec's rugged features, making him intensely male and handsome.

Leaning back against the couch, Alec sighed, the wineglass in his hand again. "You look more like an elfin sprite than that serious marine biologist I saw today," he teased. The wine was mildly fruity and semidry. Rarely had Alec had such wine, and he savored the chilled liquid.

"When I'm in the public eye, Alec, I have to present a certain kind of image."

"Why?" He motioned to her. "You look relaxed, free and beautiful. What's wrong with that image?"

Abby felt heat nettle her cheeks, and she avoided his hooded stare, more than a little aware of how womanly he made her feel. "If I showed up looking like this, a lot of Americans wouldn't take me seriously."

"Oh?"

"Unfortunately, Americans have had too many decades of prepackaged concepts. They've been brainwashed into seeing or believing only certain types of images. If you don't fit the image, then you might not be believed."

"But you dressed almost—" he searched for the right words, not wanting to insult her "—like a man. Even your hair was tamed into a severe shape."

She sighed. "I know."

"That wasn't an insult. You looked very beautiful today in your suit, but now you look like the Abby I know."

"Women have their problems in my country, Alec. Feminism isn't a new concept." When she saw the confusion in his eyes, she added, "There's a double standard in America. Women were taught they could only be housewives and mothers and that was all. In the seventies, women began to assert their rights to do anything a man can do, with the exception of certain physical limitations. Not only that, but to get equal pay for equal work." Her mouth twitched with ire. "Equal pay still hasn't happened yet, and women are continuing to be undervalued by men who run this country. Part of the answer lies in women voting for women political candidates to sway the balance of power. Only then do I think women's issues will begin to be fairly addressed."

"And so you dress like a man to be taken seriously?"

Abby was pleased with his insight. "Yes . . . exactly." She took another sip of her wine and stared down into the contents of the glass. "Every step women have taken in my country to free themselves of what men think they ought to do or be had been one hell of a struggle. The girls being born today will have it so much easier. They won't have to fight to be taken seriously as an equal, or be sexually harassed like the women before them."

"Things aren't very good in the Soviet Union for women, either," Alec noted. "A woman may be allowed to work at a job, just like a man. But she is still expected to raise the family and take care of the home, too."

She gave him a flat look. "Looks like the double standard is alive and well over there, too. Here, a woman who has a career *and* a family is referred to as a Supermom."

"A woman's life isn't easy," Alec agreed softly.

"You don't seem to have a problem with me being the way I am."

A slow smile pulled at his mouth. "How can one dislike a sunbeam?"

"Are all Soviet men like you? Poetic? Not threatened by a woman such as myself? I can't believe they are."

He shook his head. "Not many are. They see women as something to be used."

"Or abused," Abby said grimly. "Do you know that rape of women is on an alarming rise in our country? That one out of three women in the U.S. will be raped in their lifetime? And that one quarter of all girls have been sexually abused by the time they're eighteen, usually by a family member? I'll never forget those statistics. They've stuck in my mind since I heard them seven years ago. I shudder to think how much higher they've risen since then. Sad, isn't it? As women gain credibility and some equality, we have other threats to worry about.''

"That's a high price to pay," Alec said.

"The price for freedom is always high." Abby got up. "I know Lieutenant Atkin wanted me to paint a rosy picture of life in American, but I believe in telling the truth. Especially about women's rights. I'm known as a feminist, a woman who demands her rights."

Alec felt the tension in her tall, proud body. He saw the anguish in her eyes and heard the vibrating anger in her voice. "I have no idea what it's like for women in my country. To be frank, I've had little contact with that side of life."

"You're lucky. My best friend, Susan Stone, who lives across the hall from me in Washington, is a case in point." Abby came and sat down on the couch with Alec. She crossed her legs and rested her wineglass on one of her knees. "The way I met Susan four years ago was when she pounded on my apartment door at two in the morning. Her husband, Steve, was beating up on her." Abby shook her head, unable to stand the sympathy in Alec's shadowed eyes. "Susan took him to court and started divorce proceedings. To show you how sick the justice system is in our country, the damned judge decided to block the injunction to keep Steve out of the apartment. The judge, who was also a man, a part of the good-old-boy network, said Susan didn't have enough evidence as to Steve's abuse. It was her word against his. So Steve was able to stay.

"Susan asked if I'd allow her and her daughter Courtney, who was only a year old at that time, to sleep in my apartment until she could get some kind of legal protection. I said yes after hearing what had happened. When Steve got home and found out what Susan had done, he flew into a rage and started beating her up again." With a tremulous sigh, Abby whispered, "I had to take Susan to the emergency room. Alec, she had two black eyes and a broken rib. Can you believe that? I was so angry at her idiot husband that, if I'd had a gun, I'd probably have shot him."

Alec remained silent, watching the fury and hurt in Abby's face. Finally, after a minute, he murmured, "No, it's not in your blood to kill anyone."

She glanced up at him. "Don't be so sure. I can't stand men who would assault any woman or child who cannot physically defend themselves against that kind of superior strength."

He shook his head, sharing her disgust. "So what happened to your friend Susan?"

"I called the cops right away. They took one look at Susan and hauled Steve off to jail." She flashed him an angry look. "I took care of Courtney and had a lawyer friend from SOWF represent Susan. Bill got that injunction and then he went after Steve with a vengeance."

"What happened?"

"Nothing," Abby said flatly. "The judge threw out Susan's testimony in court. Can you believe that? And this isn't an isolated incident, Alec. Women go through this all over the U.S.!"

"Where is she now?"

"Susan's working very hard to be a successful stock broker in Washington, D.C. In the last three years, she's pulled herself up by her bootstraps and made something of herself."

"And Courtney?"

"Adjusting. Susan takes her to a therapist but Courtney is still wary around men. She's getting better, though."

"And this ex-husband? Is he in jail?"

Abby shook her head, so angry that she wanted to cry. "Susan divorced Steve and then he skipped town and hasn't paid a cent in alimony.

"Susan works long hours and Courtney lives half her life at day-care. When she goes to school next year, she'll be a latch-key kid, someone who goes home to an empty house because the parent has to work."

"It doesn't sound like a very healthy situation."

"You're right. But in America, both parents frequently have to work to make enough for the family to live on. Unfortunately, it's the kids who suffer."

"Has Susan fallen in love with another man?"

Sadly, Abby shook her head. "When you have something like that happen to you, Alec, it breaks your faith and trust in men in general. Not all men are like Steve, but Susan still has to learn to trust all over again, and it's not easy. No, she's single and frankly, with her work hours, she doesn't have time for a significant other."

"Significant other?"

She smiled. "A slang term for a boyfriend or a steady guy."

He shared her strained smile. "I think Susan will find a man who has her kind of strength."

"You're more hopeful than she is, that's for sure. She's grown up a lot since this thing with Steve and realizes there just aren't too many men around that she'd like to get involved with. Susan's content to wait, even if she's lonely."

"I can't disagree with her decision," Alec said. His hunger to know Abby on a personal level drove him on to ask her, "What of your family?"

She smiled softly. "I came out of a normal home, so to speak. In fact, my dad is my strongest supporter. I've inherited his tenacity and discipline."

"And your mother? How much of her is in you?"

Relaxing against the couch, Abby smiled wistfully. "I'm a lot like her in every other way. I have her red hair, although now she's got red and gray hair. She's always been a firebrand. Back in the seventies, she marched for the feminist movement and now she works part-time in Washington.

"My folks live in La Jolla, California, but my mother flies back and forth to lobby for pro-women and pro-family legislation."

"Sounds like you are from a politically active family."

Abby shrugged. "I don't consider us political at all. We're just a family who cares about our quality of life, and the future of our children and our planet. And we're willing to give our beliefs more than lip service. We go out and try to change the conditions we don't like."

Draining the last of the wine from his glass, Alec set it on the coffee table. "I like people with a commitment. On board whatever ship I served, I try to get my people involved, to care, like you do." He scowled. "Before *glasnost,* it was almost impossible because most people were afraid of the KGB spies among us. Now with this new openness, even the most diehard Communist is relenting a little, and personal expression and freedom is finally being allowed to surface."

"I just hope," Abby said with fervency, "that *glasnost* and *perestroika* are real, Alec, and not overturned."

"You think General Secretary Gorbachev is a wolf in sheep's clothing?"

Uncomfortable, Abby tried to choose her words carefully. "America has had forty years of the Cold War, Alec. Most people are distrustful of *glasnost*. Everyone wants it to work, but we're wary. But believe me, no one would love to see the nuclear race come to an end more than me."

"But . . . ?"

She smiled suddenly. "You have the most unerring way of reading my mind."

"I see the doubt register in your eyes, Abby. As an officer, it's a skill one develops to know how your men are really feeling or what they're thinking."

"In this country, there's hope that *glasnost* is for real. At the same time, there are large factions who distrust General Secretary Gorbachev. They think he's playing some kind of complex hoax to lure American into lowering its defenses." She shrugged. "I *want glasnost* to work. I think it's wonderful."

Sobering at Abby's admission, Alec said, "If it's a hoax, then I'm being fooled, too. I'm not a Communist. I never joined the Party, which is why I've been distrusted even in my position as an officer." He smiled fondly. "Fortunately; my focus has always been on the men who worked for me, not on any great goals to become an admiral in the fleet."

"Good for you. It's about time people started caring and being responsible for other people. You're a man with a heart and conscience. I didn't see that combination on the *Udaloy* among any other officers too much."

He stretched his long legs out in front of him and enjoyed the new-found freedom of Abby's country. "I'm considered a lone wolf," he said with a chuckle. "My mother has a very dry sense of humor and has passed it on to me. At school, the teachers tried to beat it out of me, but it didn't work." He flashed her a smile. "And like a wolf, I know how to hide well. I refused to lose some parts of myself after I entered the navy."

"I imagine your people benefited from it directly." Abby liked his ability to smile, unlike his Soviet counterparts who always wore such stern and unforgiving expressions. And she admired his inner strength to resist a society that obviously wanted to make clones of everyone.

Looking at her watch, Abby realized an hour had flown by. "It's eleven o'clock—you've got to be exhausted."

Alec stood when she scrambled to her bare feet. "This is the first time we've really been able to sit down and talk. I enjoyed it." The truth was, Alec had hungrily been looking forward to the time alone with Abby. She was intensely interesting to him on so many levels.

Catching his hand, she smiled and led him down the hall. "I loved it, too. Tomorrow Tim is going to take us over to a McDonald's so you can see what one looks like. It ought to be the highlight of your day," she said with a laugh. Opening the second door on the right, Abby motioned Alec through. "Your home away from home. This is your bedroom. The bathroom is on the other side of the hall. Let me get a quick shower and then it'll be all yours.''

As Abby stood in the darkened hall, her face softly shadowed, Alec had to physically stop himself from reaching out to caress the slope of her flushed cheek. ''Of course. What time do we get up tomorrow?''

''We get to sleep in, thank goodness!'' She hesitated, seeing the burning intensity in his sable eyes. Swallowing against a dry throat, Abby whispered, ''Good night, Alec. I'll see you tomorrow.''

ALEC LAY ON HIS BACK in the bed, the floral sheet and the colorful quilt up to his waist. His fingers were laced behind his head as he stared up at the ceiling. It had been an hour since he'd gotten a shower and gone to bed, but the excitement of the day was still with him, much like adrenaline coursing through his bloodstream after a demanding and exhausting naval exercise.

His mind centered gently on Abby. He liked her passion for life, her fire and her vulnerable heart. There wasn't anything that didn't touch her, he thought. When she had talked of Susan, he'd seen tears brim her eyes, as if she emphatically felt her friend's pain. And when Abby had spoken of her parents, her blue eyes danced with such life that an ache had begun in his lower body. Her hands were never still as she spoke, and she used them like a graceful ballerina to silently punctuate her speech.

The urge to lean forward, tunnel his fingers through that rich, red mass of hair that caressed her shoulders had been very real all night long.

Never had Alec been drawn as fiercely as he was to Abby. He closed his eyes and saw her mobile face, that delicate coverlet of freckles across her cheeks and nose. Her eyes shone with such life that it haunted him. Abby *was* life. A whisper of a sigh broke from his lips as he turned onto his side and allowed sleep to claim him. The coming week was going to be the best he'd ever had, he decided.

WHEN ALEC STUMBLED SLEEPILY out of his bedroom the next morning, dressed in a pair of dark brown slacks and a white cable-knit sweater, he found Abby busily cooking breakfast. Sinking down on a stool at the breakfast bar, he placed his elbows on the surface of the counter and smiled. Abby was in a pair of jeans and an apricot-colored sweater. Her hair was caught up with a white plastic clip at the back of her head and it looked like the cascading mane of a horse, decidedly provocative and appealing in his eyes.

"Good morning," he murmured.

"Oh!" Abby whirled around. Alec's sleep-ridden features and his tousled hair made him look more like a little boy than a Soviet officer. The picture made her heart beat hard in her chest, as if to underscore the magnetism he exuded. She wasn't immune to his lazy smile, hooded eyes and undoubted masculinity.

"Sorry, I didn't mean to scare you."

Abby quickly put the scrambled eggs and a rasher of bacon on a plate in front of him. "That's okay, it's just me. Here's breakfast. I was just going to wake you up."

Alec couldn't believe the eggs on the plate were real and not the powdered variety used aboard ship. As he tasted them, he was genuinely surprised. "This is very good."

Unconsciously, Abby touched her cheek, which felt hot with blush. "Thanks. I'm not a gourmet cook or anything. Mom taught me practical cooking, not fancy cooking."

Alec finished every bit of food on his plate. When Abby joined him, she had an odd-looking mixture in a bowl that sat before her.

"What's that?"

Laughing, she said, "Commonly referred to as 'rabbit food.' It's strawberry yogurt, granola and some apple chunks." She spooned up some of the yogurt and held it out to him. "Want to try it?"

The dancing merriment in her eyes couldn't be resisted, so Alec ate the offered spoonful.

Abby sat watching his expression as he munched and crunched on the food. "I don't see you hating it," she teased with a laugh.

"It's very good, this rabbit food."

"Maybe by the time you leave, I'll have turned you into a vegetarian.

Pointing to his empty plate in front of him, Alec said dryly, "I doubt it."

A knock came at the apartment door and Abby slid off the stool to answer it. Lieutenant Atkin, looking handsome in his dark blue Coast Guard uniform, smiled.

"Good morning, Dr. Fielding. May I come in?"

"Call me Abby. Yes, do come in."

Taking off his officer's cap after the door shut, he told Abby, "And you can call me Tim when we're alone." He grinned suddenly. "I don't stand on too much formality unless it's necessary."

Laughing, Abby led him to the breakfast bar. "Great! Come and sit down. Have you eaten yet?"

"No, ma'am, and I'm starved. Usually, I stop at McDonald's, but I didn't even have time to do that this morning." Tim sat down and nodded to Alec. "Good morning, sir."

With a smile in Abby's direction, to the Coast Guard officer, Alec said, "Call me Alec. I agree, formality is something to be set aside whenever possible."

Tim grinned and laid his briefcase on the counter. "Sounds good to me. Abby, I've brought copies or clippings of reports on yesterday's press conference from every major newspaper I could find. I've got to tell you—the two of you are a major happening!"

"I hope it's all good news, Tim. Just a minute, let me whip up some breakfast for you." Abby quickly made Tim a plate of scrambled eggs and fried more bacon. She saw that Alec had gulped down the bacon like a starving man, so she made him another rasher. When she placed it on Alec's plate, the grateful smile he gave her went straight to her heart. Again, her pulse bounded unevenly, and Abby realized how sensitized she was to him, to his moods and feelings. It was a pleasant discovery.

Abby came around the counter and sat on a stool between the two men. She picked up a copy of the *Washington Post*. Immediately, her brows knitted. "I knew this would happen," she said, pointing to a front-page article.

"What?" Tim asked.

"My nemesis, Dr. Monica Turner. She hates me."

Alec scowled, picking up the mug and sipping the hot coffee. "Why would anyone hate you?"

"Dr. Turner is the political advisor I told you about. The one on the International Whaling Commission who I locked horns with over whaling issues the past five years. She's more interested in the infrastructure of power than the job she's working at." She turned to Tim. "Did you read this article and the blasé communiqué issued by the White House?"

"Yes, I did," he said soberly. "Technically, I'm not supposed to take sides on this because the Coast Guard interfaces with the State Department sometimes."

"I know, I know." Abby frowned. "I can't believe the administration would take Dr. Turner's stand!"

Alec felt Abby's frustration. Her eyes flashed with the fire of anger and she slid off the stool, to pace the living room.

"Abby, I have a suggestion," Tim told her. "Off the record, of course."

She stopped. "Of course."

"Well, I think if you continue to keep the whaling issue in the news for another week or two, some major talk shows might be interested in having you come and speak about saving the whales. There's nothing like the *Oprah Winfrey Show* to get your message across. To my way of thinking, if repairs go well, the *Argonaut* will go back out to shadow that Japanese whaling fleet. Only this time, take someone from CNN and news people from the major networks who are willing to go along." His smile deepened. "If you do, I'll bet you any amount of money those talk shows will snap you up in a second when you return to Anchorage."

Abby stood there digesting Tim's plan. "That's a great idea."

"What I can do," Alec added, "is contact Captain Denisov and ask him if I can remain on board the *Argonaut* with you during the cruise—as an interested observer," he added with a slight smile. "And it doesn't hurt that I'm a navigation officer. I can help you."

Clasping her hands to her breast, Abby stared at Alec, looking so handsome in his civilian attire. "Would you? I mean, could you?"

"No promises, Abby, but I can try." Alec turned to Tim. "Would your country have a problem with this plan?"

"I can't speak for the State Department, but I don't think they're going to be able to take a position for or against your joining the *Argonaut* crew as an observer. After all, this is the period of *glasnost,* and any way to warm relations should be viewed as a step in the right direction. I'll check into it for you." Tim began to jot down notes on his ever-present note pad.

Abby rushed across the living room and threw her arms around Alec. "Thank you," she whispered in a trembling voice. "You're so wonderful."

Stunned by the sudden and unexpected contact with Abby, Alec sat there with his hands resting lightly against her waist. Her eyes had been filled with gratitude. Her skin was velvet soft against his cheek, the fragrance she wore like the scent of spices. A powerful surge of emotion shattered through his chest. As she drew away from him, he smiled up into her azure eyes, which spoke so eloquently for her. "You're welcome, *moya edinstvenaya.*"

Chapter Five

"Is McDonald's what you expected?" Abby teased Alec. They sat in a corner booth at noontime, the fast-food restaurant packed with people standing in line to give their lunch orders. Since Alec was in civilian clothes, he had gone unnoticed by most of the crowd. Tim Atkin, in uniform, sat with them and garnered a few curious looks, but nothing more.

"The food is good. Very good," Alec praised between bites of his Big Mac. He placed a third order of French fries between them on the table. "Please, eat something."

Abby took one of the cookies from the package that Tim had opened earlier for all of them and nibbled hesitantly. "I'm doing this only in the name of *glasnost,* Alec." She glanced at Tim, who sat beside her, happily eating the fries. "Aren't you even concerned about your heart or cholesterol level?"

Tim shrugged good naturedly. "I'm only twentynine, Abby. Healthy as a horse, too. I like this kind of food."

"You're both junk-food addicts," she grumbled with a shake of her head.

"Alec has good reason to eat like there's no tomorrow," Tim pointed out. "In the Soviet Union, meat is a scarce food item."

Alec nodded in agreement, his mouth full. He'd consumed two chocolate milk shakes, two orders or large French fries, and was on his second Big Mac. Looking around, he said, "I don't think my men will believe me when I tell them of this place."

"Hey, if you like this place, we ought to take you down the street to Wendy's," Tim said enthusiastically. "They've got the best chili this side of Texas."

Abby rolled her eyes. "You two are dangerous together! Tim, show a little restraint, will you? I'm not going to have Alec pigging out on junk food every day he's here. Tonight, it'll be a nice seafood dinner at a good restaurant."

"Long John Silver's has great seafood."

"Nice try, Tim, but that's another fast-food restaurant. If you two want to go there, do it, but I'm not coming with you."

"They have great coleslaw there," Tim ventured hopefully, giving her a pleading look and trying to appeal to her vegetarian nature.

With a laugh, Abby shook her head. "I'll meet you halfway. How about the Red Lobster? They've got wonderful seafood and lots of salads."

Tim stuck out his hand to her. "Deal! You drive a hard bargain, Dr. Fielding."

"My health is involved, Lieutenant. Is it any wonder I'm sticking to my guns?"

The table broke into companionable laughter. Alec wiped his fingers on the paper napkin after he was finished with his meal. "I don't remember when I've eaten so much."

Abby grinned at him. "You'd think you were starving to death." To be honest, Alec was on the thin side. He was medium boned and tall, but could easily stand another ten pounds on his frame.

Alec was starved for more than just meat. He was starved for Abby, too. She wore a short ivory-colored wool jacket over her apricot sweater and jeans. The weather was cooperating with them: cobalt-blue skies laced with cobblestoned clouds. The temperature hovered at forty, but Alec was used to that kind of cold, so it felt relatively warm to him.

Abby saw the glint in Alec's eyes and knew what he was hungry for. She felt heat rush into her cheeks. Never had she blushed so much in her whole life as when she was around Alec. The way he looked at her with those dark, brooding eyes sent her heart beating erratically. His mouth, she'd decided long ago, was the most wonderful part of him. It was a chiseled mouth with a full, lower lip. When Alec smiled, the serious planes of his face changed dramatically, and the effect literally took her breath away.

Tim glanced at the gold Rolex watch on his wrist. "Time to go, gang. Alec, we're taking you over to a newspaper office. I've got a tour of the facilities set up for you. I thought you'd like to see freedom of the press at work. Ready?''

Alec nodded and rose. He dutifully took all his paper and plastic products and put them into the waste receptacle. Abby was right behind him.

''That's another thing we Americans have to change about ourselves,'' she noted. ''Plastic isn't biodegradable and will sit for hundreds of years without breaking down in a landfill. I have a friend who is an environmental lobbyist working with fast-food restaurants trying to convince them to change from plastic to paper.''

Alec nodded. ''That would be a wise idea. Paper will break down quite quickly.''

She shook her head. ''Even you can see it, and you're a foreigner. Why can't the American people?''

''Because,'' Tim said, dumping his trash, ''we've gotten spoiled by the many social amenities at our disposal.''

''We're a disposable society, all right,'' Abby groused, following them out of the restaurant. To her delight, Alec waited for her to catch up with him, and then they walked side by side down the street. A small amount of snow was piled on the curbs from an unexpected early spring snow storm. The streets had turned slushy with the rise in temperature. Anchorage, in Abby's eyes, was a beautiful city with some of the cleanest air in the world. The mountains that surrounded the city like a crescent were wreathed in snow, the slopes covered in an emerald forest. There was no place like it on earth, and Abby dearly loved Alaska.

"Still," Alec told her, "you have much more than the average Soviet citizen. You don't have to wait in long lines to buy sparse food products. Our people must wait hours at a butcher shop, and then the meat they are able to purchase is tough and stringy."

"Sounds awful," Abby said. "On the other hand, America is into instant gratification. They used to call us the 'Me Generation.' We have to have it now. Instant food, instant success and instant money in the form of abuse of our credit cards. That's why fast-food restaurants are such a part of our culture. Everything in this country is speeding up to the point that there's no time to sit down, relax and take it easy."

Alec could well believe Abby as they walked down the wet sidewalk. He was amazed at all the cars on the highway. In Moscow, very few ordinary citizens owned cars. His attention was snagged by a huge department-store window display on their left. Everywhere Alec looked as they sauntered down the boulevard were retail outlets.

"You don't have lines of people waiting to get into this clothing store," he noted, slowing down and looking at the mannequins in the window display.

Abby halted beside him. "No. Should we?"

"In Moscow, our stores are nearly empty of consumer goods, and what little there is, we must stand

in lines to try and buy.'' He pointed to the mannequins. There was awe in his voice as he asked, ''Are
those American jeans?''

Tim moved beside Alec. ''Yes, they are.''

''How much are they?''

Abby enjoyed watching Alec's delight. ''After
we're finished with the newspaper tour, why don't we
come back over here and let you do a little shopping? It's a real American thing to do.'' She smiled
at him. '' 'Shop till you drop' is our slogan!''

''I THINK,'' ABBY TEASED Alec as they entered her
apartment that evening, ''that you've had a great
day.'' She hefted a large package to the other arm
and closed the door after he'd entered with his own
parcels in hand.

Grinning, Alec placed all the items on the floor
near the couch. ''I've just spent three months' worth
of pay.''

''You'd put the women of Rodeo Drive in Hollywood to shame, Alec.'' Abby placed her packages
next to his on the floor. He'd gone back into J.C.
Penney after touring the newspaper facility and
bought six pairs of jeans. Interestingly enough, Alec
had bought only two pairs for himself, but had gotten the other pairs as gifts for friends. Jeans from the
West, he told her excitedly, were the hit of the Soviet
black market and sold for an enormous amount of
rubles. Alec wasn't a selfish man, and that endeared
him even more to Abby. She'd talked him into sev-

eral collegiate-design shirts to wear with his jeans, but he refused to buy a business suit. He had nowhere on the *Udaloy* to keep that amount of clothing, storage space was at a premium.

Abby had seen Alec looking fondly at a pair of cowboy boots at a shoe store after they'd left Penney's. Knowing Alec was enamored of America's Western and Native American heritage, she bought them for him. The look on his face, the gratefulness combined with some undefined but heated emotion, had been her return gift.

Tim had seen Alec looking at a Levi's denim jacket at a boutique toward the end of their shopping spree. Out of the goodness of his heart, he'd bought it as a gift for Alec—out of his own pocket, not the Coast Guard's. Abby wanted to hug Tim for his generosity because Alec had wanted the jacket so badly, but couldn't afford it on his meager paycheck. He hadn't come to America with very much money.

Alec sauntered into the kitchen later after putting all his packages into the guest bedroom. He sat down on the bar stool. It was nearly 10:00 p.m., and he watched Abby pour them each a small glass of blush wine. Smiling, she remained on her side of the counter, opposite him.

"You'll be the hit of the *Udaloy* in your American clothes when you go back aboard."

He smiled and sipped the wine. "It will probably cause nothing but envy and I'll have to watch to make sure they aren't stolen. I have several old and dear friends of our family back in Moscow who will treasure the jeans I'll send to them as soon as I get back on board the ship.''

''You'll make a lot of people happy. So, how do you like America so far?''

''There isn't anything to dislike about it. Your country is so different from the Soviet Union.'' With a shake of his head, Alec murmured, ''And all that food at the Red Lobster...and no waiting in lines. Is this the way it is in the United States?''

She nodded. ''I wish you could come with me to Washington, D.C. There're posh restaurants, a million things to do and many more places to see. I like cities because of what they offer, but I prefer country living. My apartment is in McLean, Virginia, and is secluded in a lovely grove of elm and oak trees. There're honeysuckle bushes growing all around the building. I've got a bottom apartment, a small enclosed area with a tiny lawn and flowers planted around the border of it. When I'm not there, Susan takes care of my place.''

''She is the best kind of friend,'' Alec said.

''I just wish...''

Alec cocked his head. ''What?''

''Oh, I just wish Susan could meet someone like Tim Atkin. He's such a nice guy, Alec. So gentlemanly, and he's so warm and personable. And—'' Abby grinned ''—he doesn't have a girlfriend.''

"I thought he told me he was stationed at Coast Guard headquarters in Washington, D.C.," Alec said.

Abby's eyes widened. "He is? Tim's from Washington?"

With a laugh, Alec said, "Are you going to be...how do you say it? A matchmaker?"

Excitedly, Abby stood there thinking. "Tim isn't married, and I just know Susan would like him! Oh, what an opportunity! I even have a picture of her! I think I'll drop a few hints tomorrow and see how Tim reacts to Susan's photo." Rubbing her hands, she grinned over at Alec. "I'm a real matchmaker when I want to be."

"You'll get no argument from me. I've seen the way you go after something you want."

Trying to look contrite, Abby said, "Well, Alec, Susan really deserves someone as nice as Tim. Don't you think?"

He shrugged. "I've always believed in fate. If two people are to meet, that is how it will be."

"Look how we met," she teased.

Alec's face dimpled. "Yes, and I don't ever regret it."

"Not for a second? Not even when you were freezing to death in that water trying to save my hide?"

He shook his head. "*Moya edinstvenaya,* I have no regrets. Not one..." Except that time was not on their side. Alec ached to stay with Abby, to explore her, to get to know her on so many different levels. Today, she had been a delightful child at Penney's, and he'd never laughed so much or so hard or for so long. She brought out the sunlight he'd kept closely guarded within himself.

Abby frowned. "That's the second time you've called me that in Russian. What does it mean?"

"Do you think it's a cuss?"

Today, Alec found out a great deal more about American lingo, including the timber, fishing and mining men of Alaska he encountered as they walked around Anchorage. At a small bar, a couple of bearded fishermen were tossing vile language at one another just as Alec, Tim and Abby walked by. Tim had to delicately explain what all the words meant.

Abby laughed. "Listen, under no circumstances would I believe an officer in the Soviet navy would ever curse a blue streak like those two guys did in front of that bar."

"Don't be so sure. When we're on military exercises, believe me, cursing becomes a regular part of our language at times." He saw surprise in Abby's dancing blue eyes. Unconsciously, he reached for her hand and cradled it momentarily. "But what I called you isn't a curse word. It is an affectionate term, one used for someone special."

Shaken by Alec's unexpected touch, Abby stood very still. She stared down at the long, spare fingers that had captured her hand. A part of her wondered what it would be like to kiss Alec, to taste and expe-

rience his strength and intensity. Abruptly, Abby
tried to stop the feeling, but couldn't. She melted
beneath his warm sable gaze as he gently held her
hand.

"What does it mean, then?" she asked, her voice
suddenly husky with emotion.

"My only one." He turned her hand over and
studied it intently. "You're so delicate, Abby. You
have the hand of an artist, someone of great sensitivity, and yet, you have the courage of the bear to
stand up to a Japanese whaler in a trawler that's
twenty times smaller." Not wanting to release her, yet
knowing he must, Alec did so. Her cheeks were
flaming red, her lips were parted, and surprise was
etched in her eyes. Yet, Alec also saw something else
in them, a luster that told him she liked his touch.

Abby suddenly felt bereft as Alec reluctantly released her hand. Her flesh tingled where his fingers
had rested. She licked her lower lip and tried to re-
cover from his unexpected intimacy. "I—uh, that's
a lovely name." The words he'd spoken so softly had
touched her heart, her soul. There was no way she
could mistake the meaning of those words because
the look in his eyes was one of heat and longing.

The tension in his body made Alec very aware of
how Abby affected him physically. More than once
he'd wondered what it would be like to have her in
his arms. Would she be as passionate a lover as her
red hair proclaimed? Would she be as sensitive as her
eyes promised? *Yes, to both questions,* his heart an-

swered. Her response to his holding her hand had been telling. For all her courage and bravado, she was hauntingly vulnerable in the world of human relationships, and that made him want her with a fierceness that consumed him like a storm at sea.

Shaken himself, Alec whispered, "I think it's time I got ready for bed."

"Yes . . ."

Abby pretended to busy herself in the kitchen. She heard Alec get up from the stool and leave. Turning, she stood leaning against the kitchen counter, her heart hammering. His touch had made her pulse skyrocket. His action had been unexpected. Molten. As she put the wine bottle away, Abby tried to make logical sense of what had occurred. She couldn't. *My only one.* Did Russians use certain terms like Americans used certain buzz words that really didn't mean much at all? Was it a shallow term? Not according to the look in Alec's eyes and the low timbre of his voice when he'd whispered it to her. Abby wished she knew for sure, one way or another.

"ALEC, YOUR REQUEST TO act as an observer aboard the *Argonaut* for a week following its repairs has been approved." Tim handed Alec a set of orders. "We just received this dispatch from Captain Denisov aboard the *Udaloy*. He's cleared your request right up to the Kremlin and back. I'm impressed."

Abby gasped and walked over to where the two men stood near the apartment door. Tim had arrived at 9:00 a.m., looking resplendent, as usual, in his dark blue uniform. Alec smiled down at her and showed her the orders.

"Well, can you put up with me one more week?" Alec asked her.

Reading the document, Abby grew excited. "Of course! Tim, isn't this wonderful? Do you know what this means?"

Tim grinned. "Yes, ma'am, I do. I've already got things in motion. I've contacted the four major networks, and you're going to have cameramen and reporters from three of them. They'll be taping what you do out there on the Bering Sea and sending the video stateside on a daily basis."

Thrilled, Abby clapped her hands. "I'll bet Dr. Turner is going to strip gears when she finds out what's happened! The humpback whales are going to get national attention again!"

"Better," Tim added, "is the fact that Moscow has approved of Alec's being aboard the *Argonaut* as an official observer. The Soviet Union has already signed an agreement not to hunt the whales, so this is really going to add importance to what you're going to be doing."

"Do you think any of the major talk shows will be interested after that week at sea?" Abby asked, holding her breath.

"I've already got Oprah Winfrey's assistant agreeing to have you and Alec on her program. I'm working on three other talk shows right now."

Shocked, Abby looked up at Alec. "You mean he can come with me to do these talk shows?"

Tim pointed to the orders. "Alec has been given a total of three weeks with us. I talked to Captain Stratman this morning, and he said it will be another four days before the *Argonaut* is seaworthy again. Then, you'll spend seven days at sea, and after that, we'll take you stateside for the talk-show circuit."

Abby threw her arms around Tim. "You're such a public-relations genius, I could kiss you!" Releasing him from the embrace, Abby stepped back and asked, "You will be going to sea with us, won't you?"

Tim shook his head. "Officially, I can't go aboard the *Argonaut* because that would symbolically be siding with the SOWF on this issue, and the Coast Guard can't do that. However, I'll be here in Anchorage assisting you and the networks' personnel in every way possible."

"How about the talk shows? You'll be with us then, won't you?"

"Yes, ma'am. I wouldn't miss that opportunity for the world. I'll be coordinating everything from behind the scenes for you. Alec is an official guest of the U.S., and the Coast Guard has been chosen to be his escort and host."

Alec laughed because he knew exactly what Abby had in mind. She looked up at him and smiled.

"Tim, I just happened to have a photo of my best and dearest friend, Susan Anderson. You know, she lives in Washington, D.C. Let me show you a picture of her...."

Alec stood aside and watched Abby beautifully demonstrate her ability to matchmake. It was obvious that Tim was fully taken by the photo of Susan, and he didn't seem to mind that she had a four-year-old daughter and was divorced. Abby wisely let Tim keep the photo—for the time being.

Dressed in his new pair of jeans, his collegiate-looking long sleeved white-and-blue-striped shirt and his denim jacket, Alec waited for Abby to grab her coat. Tim was going to take them to a fish hatchery and on a tour of the wharf area.

As they left the apartment, Alec smiled. "Do you think we'll meet more fishermen with colorful cuss words down at the wharf?"

Abby rolled her eyes. "It's hard to tell, Alec." She glanced at Tim, who walked at her side. "If we do, Tim will tell you what all the words mean, won't you?"

The officer grinned and a flush crept across his freckled cheeks. He pulled out a compact paperback dictionary from the pocket of his dark blue overcoat. "Here, Alec. A gift from me to you. This is a Russian/English dictionary I bought for you last night from a B. Dalton bookstore. It's the most up-to-date one I could find, and it has a lot of slang words we use in it. If you hear any new curse words, you can look them up in there first. If you can't find them, then I'll explain what they mean.''

Delighted with Tim's strategy, Abby just knew that Susan would like the Coast Guard officer. Tonight, when they got home after a long and exciting day of showing Alec more of Anchorage, Abby was going to call her best friend. After all, Susan should know what her friend was planning to do when she got back to Washington.

''DOESN'T IT ALL SOUND wonderful, Susan?'' Abby sat on her bed, the Princess phone next to her on the mattress. It was 7:00 p.m. in Alaska and midnight on the East Coast. Fortunately, Susan hadn't gone to bed yet.

''I don't know, Abby.''

''Tim's so cute. He's such an officer and a gentleman. Completely unlike Steve.''

''I'll have to think about it.''

''You've never dated a military man,'' Abby pointed out enthusiastically. ''Just those greedy stockbrokers you work with, and you found out a long time ago that you didn't like their kind.''

''I won't date them. They're so self-centered. My boss is pushing all the account executives to jump on the junk-bond bandwagon, and I've refused to get involved. I'm getting a lot of pressure from my boss to sell them to my clients, but I just don't feel good about it. The stock market has done nothing but continue to break records, and I know there's a downturn coming. I can feel it in my bones. I'm trying to protect my investors, not get them to take unnecessary risks."

"Then don't do it."

"I'm not sure I can keep my job if I don't, Abby."

"Damn." Abby chewed on her lower lip, thinking for a moment. "Sometimes I think it would be nice if women who wanted to could go back to the fifties and be housewives and mothers. You're like that. All you wanted to do was get married and have a family."

Susan laughed sourly. "Yeah, and look what it got me. No thanks, I'd rather stay a yuppie, be a supermom and cope with home life alone than to get married for the convenience of a second paycheck coming into the household. I'd have to live with the guy and frankly, Abby, I haven't found the men out there to be that stellar. I'd give anything to find a guy who can laugh, cry and talk with me."

"I keep telling you—I've found him! Lieutenant Tim Atkin is the one, Susan! Believe me!"

"I don't know, Abby. Every guy I've dated has been a bust. They figure if they take you to dinner, you owe them something afterward. That's outrageous! I won't do it! And then, on top of everything else, with the AIDs epidemic..."

Abby hung on to her patience. She knew Susan had a right to feel as she did about men. Abby's own experience with men had been positive, but she couldn't disagree that a lot of men weren't the kind of marriage material she'd want, either. "Tim is warm, open, honest and incredibly sensitive."

"Then why isn't he married?"

"He's been busy with his career, I suppose, but I really don't know."

"Precisely my point. The guy's got some kind of flaw, then, regardless of what you see in him."

"No, I just can't believe that. Susan, you know how good my instincts are about people. The moment I met Tim, I knew he was a wonderful guy. He really liked the photo of you."

"Does he know about Courtney?"

"Yes, he's seen Courtney, and Tim thinks she's the most beautiful little girl he's ever seen. So there!"

"He's probably lying through his teeth just to not upset you."

Giving a little laugh, Abby said, "Susan, I love you, pessimism and all. When the time comes, let me invite you two over for dinner and introduce you to Tim, okay? If you don't like him, it's no big deal. But if you do—"

"One step at a time, Abby. That's all I can handle with my work load and Courtney. I'm having troubles with the day-care center, and I'm probably going to have to find another one. Everything's so expensive. I work twelve hours a day at that office, barely get home in time to cook Courtney dinner and spend a half hour of quality time with her before I've got to go to my office here at home and work until midnight. If I can't find a reasonably priced day-care center, I don't know what I'm going to do."

Frowning, Abby nodded. She hurt for her friend and realized that many single mothers were in the same boat and many times, worse off than Susan. "Nothing says life is fair."

"I know it isn't!" Susan laughed. "Hey, enough of my troubles. How are *you?* You haven't said a thing. I saw that gorgeous looking Soviet officer, Captain Alec Rostov. What a hunk, Abby! My God, are you constantly drooling when you're around him?"

Giggling, Abby said, "No, but I should be. He's terribly good-looking, isn't he?"

"Do his dark good looks match the man inside, though?"

With a sigh, Abby laid back on the pillows she'd arranged behind her. "Oh, Susan, he's wonderful."

"Wonderful. You use that word all the time, Abby, to describe everything."

"Well, he is! He's got a dry sense of humor, he's very open and honest about how he feels and he has an honor about him that's hard to match in any other man I've ever met."

"Sounds serious."

"Nonsense."

"Abby, I hear that wistful sound in your voice. As long as I've known you, and met your significant others from time to time, I've never heard that tone in your voice before."

"You're hearing things," Abby said, then she went on to tell Susan about the three weeks that Alec was going to remain stateside with her and the whale-protection efforts.

"Awesome," Susan whispered after hearing about the entire plan. "This Lieutenant Atkin sure sounds like a can-do man."

"He really is, Susan. I'll bet the guy ends up as commandant of the Coast Guard someday with the way he gets things done."

"Well . . . maybe I should pencil in some time for this dinner you're proposing."

"Great! Well, Supermom, I'll let you go."

"Listen, you be careful out at sea, Abby. That Russian hunk won't always be around to save your rear."

"If I get into trouble, he'll be right at my side," Abby assured her gently. "Give Courtney a hug and kiss for me, will you? And I'll be in touch. Believe me, I know you're going to like Tim."

Laughing, Susan whispered dramatically, "You never give up, do you, Abby? Always the idealist. The one who believes in right, goodness and positive endings. I love you. Take care."

Abby hung up the receiver and placed the phone back on the bedstand, then sat on her bed, thinking. She hurt for Susan, for all the bad things that had happened to her. Nothing had gone right in her personal life since the divorce. The few men she'd dated were selfish and only wanted her for one thing: sex.

Abby knew not all men were like that. Susan had yet to have an experience with one of those kind of men. Tim, she felt, was just what Susan needed. If only she could get them together, Abby knew it would work.

Smoothing out the goose-down comforter around her, she mulled over Susan's other comments. Abby wondered if her voice had grown wistful when she talked about Alec. Every day spent around him made her feel as if some kind of bonding were continuing to take place. She could feel it, that subtle, delicious tension that had always been strung between them from the first moment she'd become conscious and seen him sitting at her bedside.

As Abby closed her eyes and took a deep, steadying breath, flashes of the past two days shuttered across her lids. They were all of Alec, his expressions, the heated looks he'd give her when he didn't think she was watching him, his engaging smile. There was such stability about him, such quiet, calm confidence. All of those things appealed greatly to her. And on top of it all, he'd saved her life. Was she merely feeling this way out of gratefulness? Or were her electric emotions that leapt every time he touched her or looked at her caused by something else?

No man had ever affected Abby this way. Confused, she sighed and slowly got off the bed. Next week they'd be on board the *Argonaut*. Abby hungered for the sea again, to go back and protect her whales. She also looked forward to the time when they could be alone, truly alone, on board the ship. Private time with Alec had been at a premium, and she had so much she wanted to ask of him, explore with him. Yes, being on the *Argonaut* would be a very special time with a very special man.

Chapter Six

"Abby, be careful out there."

Abby forced a slight smile for Alec. She felt the firm strength of his hand on her arm as she stood on the lurching, wet deck of the *Argonaut,* out in the Bering Sea. No more than half a mile away was a Japanese whaling fleet consisting of the factory ship and eight catcher ships. It was the catchers that actively hunted the humpback whales now visible a few miles away from the *Argonaut.* The catchers were smaller, faster ships, designed for killing the whales. Once a whale was harpooned, it was taken to the factory ship, where it was cut up and stored.

Brad, the SOWF photographer, was preparing to have an inflatable rubber Zodiac put over the side of the salmon trawler. This would be the first show-down with the Japanese fleet in the *Argonaut's* three days at sea. The early-May afternoon was gray, and it would soon start to rain. Abby would be steering the Zodiac, keeping it between the fleeing pod of humpback whales and the catcher ships ready to start firing their harpoons.

"I'll be very careful," she promised.

"Abby! We're ready," Brad called.

Glancing to the left, she saw the Zodiac in the grayish-green water, Brad sitting in the craft, holding it close to the trawler. Waves were four and five feet high in a confused sea, a dangerous combination when trying to ease the motor-driven Zodiac through the surrounding pattern.

"I've got to go, Alec."

Reluctantly, he released her arm. Abby was dressed in a bulky bright orange survival suit in case she was dumped into the frigid Artic water, and a life vest to keep her afloat. Alec saw the fear lurking in her eyes, but he also saw the determination in the set of her lovely mouth. The past three days had been close to heaven in his opinion. Although representatives of three major networks were on board, he and Abby had still had peace and quiet at night, each sleeping alone, their cabins next to the other's.

As Abby entered the bobbing, bucking Zodiac, Alec leaned over the rail. On either side of him, video cameras from the networks were taking pictures.

"Abby!" he shouted.

Her head jerked up.

"Stay safe, *moya edinstvenaya.*"

She grinned and lifted her mittened hand. Her heart swelled with a fierce tidal wave of feeling. Every day had brought her closer and closer to Alec in a subtle but powerful way. He had brought a wealth of unknown emotions into the fabric of her life.

Brad was situated in the center of the Zodiac and threw her a thumbs-up. The small engine on the Zodiac sputtered and then roared to life, and Abby guided the small boat away from the lee of the *Argonaut*. The last thing she saw as they headed around the bow was Alec's darkened features beneath the trooper cap he wore with his uniform. His mouth was grimly set, and he was gripping the rail of the trawler, watching her. As she carefully read the confused wave direction, zigzagging around the swells, her heart and focus were divided between Alec and her whales.

Ahead Abby could see the geysers of spray that the huge, barnacled humpbacks were releasing as they surfaced to gulp in another volume of fresh air. Coming up steadily behind them was a catcher ship. She looked up at the vessel, the steel-barbed harpoon readied to be fired. Brad not only manned the video camera wrapped in plastic to keep it dry from the water as they dodged the waves, but the radio as well.

As they zigzagged in front of the catcher, the massive prow of the whaler rose and fell within four hundred yards of the Zodiac. Abby knew if the engine on the Zodiac failed, they'd be smashed within moments by that bow. Heart pounding, she carefully kept her Zodiac placed between the catcher and the pod of whales. In this group, Abby counted four males, five females and five three-month-old calves. As if the adult humpbacks realized they were in danger, they had placed the babies between them, so that the pod fanned out in a semicircle, like a crescent moon, so that the calves provided less of a target. Because of the calves, the pod couldn't move at the full twelve-knot speed of which an adult humpback is capable. They were easy targets for the Japanese.

"Abby," Brad shouted, "they're preparing to launch the first harpoon!"

Lifting her wet face, Abby wiped the brine away. More water droplets were flung across the Zodiac as it was caught by a wave. The Zodiac lifted, shifted and then slid into a trough. Brad clung to the anchored radio unit in the center of the craft in order not to be thrown overboard. Abby flattened herself so that the Zodiac wouldn't tip over.

Jerking her chin up, Abby glanced over her shoulder. The catcher was angling to the left. Quickly, she turned the Zodiac to intercept the catcher. A wave caught her as she raced to place the craft between the harpoon and the whales.

"Better hurry!" Brad shouted, catching the action with the video camera that rested on his shoulder.

Would the Japanese fire the harpoon? In the past week and a half, they'd suffered worldwide condemnation through the press for what they'd done to the *Argonaut*. The U.S. had officially ignored Captain Stratman's charges against the Japanese, so nothing had been done to punish the catcher ship for ramming the *Argonaut*. With this particular whaling fleet, Abby had no guarantee that this catcher would back off and hunt another day. She tried to prepare herself for the eventuality that the catcher would ram them in order to harpoon the fleeing humpbacks.

If the harpoon was fired, it could conceivably strike the Zodiac or the occupants. If the harpoon did slam into the Zodiac, Abby knew the craft would sink immediately. She or Brad might be killed or injured. Staring up at the rusty harpoon less than six hundred yards away, Abby's throat tightened with tension.

Ahead of her, she could hear the whales blowing. Constantly having to dodge the erratic waves and try to ensure the Zodiac wouldn't be caught and flipped, Abby had to also keep an eye on the catcher. It was a deadly dance between her, the sea and the ship.

"Abby, there's an ice floe ahead! If the whales make that, the Japanese can't follow them!" Brad crowed loudly across the roar of the craft.

Squinting, Abby could barely make out the ice floe. It was at least five miles away. Too far.

"Watch it!" Brad yelled.

Eyes moving to the catcher, Abby saw the ship changing direction once again, to get a good firing angle on the pod. The loaded harpoon was now being aimed directly at them, or more specifically, at a cow and her calf, who were decidedly lagging behind the rest of the pod just ahead of the Zodiac. Heartbeat increasing, Abby realized with a sinking feeling that the small calf had tired and was trying to rest. The mother was gently nudging him along, but he simply wanted to rest and not swim.

"Brad, call the *Argonaut!*" Abby shouted. "Tell them we're staying to protect this mother and calf from the fleet!"

Alec was on the bridge with Captain Stratman when the call came in over the radio.

"Damn," Stratman growled. He clenched the pipe between his teeth, heaving the *Argonaut* to port and heading directly toward where the Zodiac that was moving around in a slow circle to protect the whales.

"What are you going to do?" Alec demanded.

"Try to warn that catcher to move off," he said grimly. The *Argonaut* shifted and Stratman pointed the bow directly at the Japanese ship.

Holding on to the brass railing inside the bridge, Alec watched tautly. Abby was holding her position near the mother and calf. The catcher was bearing down on them at full speed. "He doesn't care if you're here or not, Captain. You'd better have another plan of attack."

"I can't put myself between him and Abby! He'll ram me again."

Alec's eyes narrowed. "You can't afford *not* to put your ship between them. That catcher will strike both the Zodiac and the whales if you don't."

Stratman flashed Alec an irritated look. On the bridge with them were all the news crews, their Minicams rolling. In a lowered voice, he told his first mate, Gary Gent, "You order Abby out of the area. Let those bastards have the whales! Tell her I can't protect her. We talked about this before she went out, that I wouldn't put my ship in jeopardy again. She knew, dammit!"

"Yes, sir!" Gent replied, getting on the radio immediately.

"John," Brad radioed back, his voice strained, "Abby is refusing to leave. Repeat, we aren't leaving. Abby wants these whales protected. Over."

"Damn," Stratman whispered under his breath. "Gent, tell 'em I ain't gonna risk this vessel! If I become a wedge, that catcher will ram us to smithereens. Tell her that and tell her to get the hell out of there!"

Alec's grip on the brass rail tightened. He could see the positions of the players involved. The Japanese ship was rapidly closing the distance. Abby again refused to move and leave the whales as targets. The only ship that could make a difference and save both the whales and the Zodiac was the *Argonaut*.

"Captain, you've *got* to put your ship between Abby and the catcher," Alec said tensely.

"No way. I ain't gonna risk this ship. Insurance is paying for repairs this time, but they said they won't if it happens again." He pointed an angry finger in the direction of the catcher. "Dammit, this guy plays for keeps! This particular fleet ain't like the rest of the whaling fleets we've encountered. The rest have all backed down, but he ain't going to!"

Abby's life was at stake, and so was Brad's. Alec glared at the small man. There was no time left. A decision had to be made.

"Give me the helm, Captain Stratman," Alec ordered coolly.

"What?"

"Let me assume command."

Stratman's eyes widened enormously. "You're outa your mind if—"

Alec shoved his face into the captain's face. "Stratman, you get on the radio to that Japanese catcher. You tell him an officer from the Soviet navy has taken over command of your trawler. You tell him if he wants to risk ramming me, he's ramming the Soviet Union. I can make life so miserable for him politically that it will make tangling with that Zodiac look like child's play. This is an international incident in the making. I don't think that captain will risk it. Now do it!"

Gripping the wheel, Alec watched as Stratman leapt aside. Instantly, the American captain was on the radio, screaming at the Japanese catcher. Wrenching the *Argonaut* tightly to port, Alec aimed the bow directly into the oncoming waves. There was little time. Very little. The tension was palpable on the bridge. Alec had not forgotten about the news teams on the bridge. He was risking his navy career, and worse, possible censure by his government for taking this action. He didn't care. If Abby was courageous enough, foolish enough, to try to save the mother and calf, then someone had to rise to the occasion and equal her bravery. She deserved nothing less.

The radio traffic increased markedly. Alec kept the trawler pointed directly between the Zodiac and the catcher. Stratman was screaming into the microphone, and Alec could hear the Japanese skipper shrieking back. Threats moved heatedly back and forth across the airwaves. Alec steadied the trawler, less than half a mile from where the Zodiac bobbed on the restless ocean.

"They ain't gonna do it!" Stratman roared. "They don't give a damn about an international incident! The captain said he's in international waters and those whales are fair game!"

"Fine," Alec ground out softly. He swung the helm rapidly, the *Argonaut*'s bow aimed directly at the catcher bearing down on them less than a mile away. "Then that captain is going to have to ram us."

"What?" Stratman croaked in disbelief. "Not with my ship, you ain't!"

Alec swung on him, his voice angry. "Captain, get a hold of yourself. Where are your priorities? What's important here? An old scow or two people's lives?"

Stratman glared at him and then at the cameras. "Shut those damn things off!"

"Sorry," one newswoman said, "you agreed to let us tape, Captain. I can't."

Swinging around, Stratman hissed at Alec, "They'll sink us!"

Alec shook his head. "No, they won't. When I get in position, I want you to make a call to the skipper of that catcher. Tell him the *Argonaut* has suddenly developed engine trouble and we're dead in the water." Alec grimly watched the ship approaching. "Tell him we've got newspeople on board and they're recording this confrontation. If he rams a vessel dead in the water, his license as a sea captain is as good as gone, and he knows that. No, he won't risk his license."

Shaking his head, Stratman muttered, "Rostov, you've got more cards up your sleeve than a damned Las Vegas poker player."

"Is that a compliment or insult?"

Grabbing the microphone, Stratman snarled, "You take it any way you want! You're responsible for the outcome of this situation!"

Sweat stood out on Alec's upper lip. He wiped it away with the back of his hand. He leaned over, pulling both engine throttles back to idle position. "Make that call now." Jockeying the throttles gingerly with one hand, Alec made sure the *Argonaut* stayed between Abby and the catcher.

The catcher had a full head of steam, and Alec knew it would take at least half a mile for the ship to change course. They were less than a mile apart now. He keyed his hearing to Stratman, but kept his attention on the position of the *Argonaut* and the direction of the waves.

"He's mad," Stratman declared after giving the Japanese skipper the story.

"That's his problem," Alec said dryly. His long fingers remained tense across the throttles, playing them gently, keeping the bow in the direction of the catcher. "Look back. What's Abby doing?"

Stratman craned a look over his shoulder. "She's still circling that mother and calf."

Alec didn't expect Abby to back down. He knew she wouldn't. He didn't want her to. "Demand the skipper give you an answer, Captain."

"Give the guy some time to think about this, will you?" Stratman exploded. "You just can't keep pushing like this!"

In a steel tone, Alec whispered, "The way you win a situation like this is to be more aggressive than the other party, Captain. Make the call."

Grumpily, Stratman called the Japanese skipper once again.

Alec knew the catcher was coming up on the point of no return. He stared hard at the bow of the whaler. If it didn't begin to move to one side or the other, then he was faced with a real crisis. He couldn't afford to allow Stratman's trawler to be rammed. And he couldn't allow Abby or Brad to be killed, either. Sweat dripped from him, soaking into the fabric of his uniform.

"Look!" a newswoman cried triumphantly, "the catcher's turning! He's turning!"

A collective sigh crossed the bridge. Alec grinned tightly. Stratman put down the microphone and glared at him.

"You sure you ain't Irish, Rostov?"

"No, Captain. Why do you ask?"

"Because you've got the luck of one, that's why."

Playing the throttles, Alec said, "Abby's got the Irish blood. It's her luck that's helped us."

Taking off his cap, Stratman wiped his sweaty forehead. "Whew, this is gettin' too rough out here."

Alec said nothing, watching as the entire Japanese fleet slowly made a turn and headed south. "Radio Abby and tell her the good news," he ordered Stratman, "and then, you can have the helm. I'm going down to help them back on board."

"THE JAPANESE FLEET IS heading back to Japan," Alec told Abby after she'd changed into dry clothes. She wore a bulky knit emerald-green sweater and an almost threadbare pair of jeans and tennis shoes. He stood with her in the passageway between their cabins, braced against the constant motion of the *Argonaut*.

"That's great!" she exclaimed.

In the low light provided by a few bulbs set into the wood ceiling, Alec saw that despite Abby's enthusiasm, she was exhausted. He reached out, gently grazing her smooth, flushed cheek. "You're tired. Why don't you rest for a while, Abby?"

A soft sigh escaped her lips as Alec's thumb brushed her skin. Abby waited for such times as this, their private moments, the unguarded moments away from the press's prying cameras. His quiet strength had given her so much during the past week. Lifting her eyelashes, she gazed up into his rugged, shadowed face, hotly aware of the burning light in his dark eyes.

"In a little while, Alec. Let me go up and talk to John, first. He seemed awfully upset over what I did. I owe him an explanation for my decision, plus an apology for what I did."

With a partial smile, Alec forced himself to stop caressing her cheek. She enjoyed his touch as much as he needed to touch her. "You'd better contact Tim, too. If the Japanese fleet is returning home, that means our mission is over and we can return to Anchorage sooner than expected. I think your news people got the story they were hoping to get."

Abby agreed, exhausted. "That means we'll find out how many talk shows want us to go on and speak about the whale and dolphin issues."

"Yes."

"Okay, I'll do that, and then I'll rest. If I go to sleep, will you wake me up in time for dinner?" Abby glanced at her watch. "That's two hours away."

"I will," Alec promised. He watched her turn and moved quietly down the passageway toward the bridge ladder. There was such grace to Abby, her shoulders proudly thrown back, her spine straight and made of nothing but raw courage. Wanting to get a few hours of privacy, Alec returned to his own cabin.

A KNOCK ON HER CABIN DOOR awakened Abby with a start. Groggy, she muttered, "Come in...." How long had she slept? Looking at her watch, she realized it was nearly 8:00 p.m. Just as she threw off the blanket and sat up on the bunk attached to the bulkhead, she saw Alec enter with a tray of food.

"I thought I'd better wake you so you could eat," he said, shutting the cabin door.

Rubbing her face tiredly, Abby nodded. She patted the bunk. "Bring it over here. It feels like the sea has settled down quite a bit."

Alec sat and then transferred the tray to Abby's lap. Eating on a rolling, pitching boat was an art. "The waves are running one to two feet, almost smooth." He handed her the napkin and flatware.

"Thanks," she murmured huskily. "Oh, good, you got me coffee. I feel so groggy."

Abby's hair was deliciously mussed from sleeping. Alec took several strands and moved them gently away from her face and across her shoulders. "Adrenaline letdown," he explained. "After a high-stress time, the body uses up its energy source and you've got to sleep afterward to recoup."

Alec's touch was evocative. "You're obviously no stranger to adrenaline highs," she said, digging in hungrily to the food. Brad, who doubled as the cook on board, knew she loved pasta and had made vegetarian spaghetti for her tonight along with some crusty garlic toast.

Resting his elbows on his knees, his hands draped casually between his legs, Alec nodded. "Life on board a Soviet warship is never dull. We're constantly training."

Abby gave him a glance, munching on the toast. "John told me what happened on the bridge when Brad and I were out in the Zodiac."

Alec twisted a look in her direction. "I did what I felt was needed to keep both of you safe, Abby."

"John was pretty upset with you."

"I was upset with him. He put more care into this boat than two human beings."

She watched the changing shadows across his serious features and heard the emotionally charged commitment in his tone. "One of the reporters ran the entire video sequence for me in her cabin." Abby's voice grew husky. "You're really something else, Alec Rostov. If they show any part of that clip back in the States, you're going to come off like the old-fashioned hero.''

He had the good grace to blush. "It wasn't a pre-meditated act of heroism on my part, Abby. I knew you weren't going to leave the whales open to harpooning by that catcher. I agreed with your decision. If this old scow had been mine, I'd have done a great deal more than I did, believe me."

"I just wish you knew how special you are, Alec."

"Is it necessary I know?" he asked philosophically. "The only person I care about and what she thinks of me is you."

Abby sat very still, digesting his admission. "When I was out there, I was scared to death, Alec. As we were circling the mother and calf, I kept having flashbacks of last time, when we'd gotten rammed and I was tossed overboard." She avoided his sharpened gaze, and her voice grew hoarse. "I was afraid I was going to die this time, and I didn't want to. As that catcher bore down on us and didn't look like it was going to change direction in time, I really got in touch with what was important in life for me." She put the tray aside.

Gently, Alec took her hand and held it between his own. "What did you discover?"

Tears made her vision blur. "My commitment to the whales and dolphins is stronger than my fear of death, that's one thing I found out." She wiped her tears away with her fingers and then gave him a shy look. "I cry a lot. It's just me."

"Crying is healthy," Alec whispered.

Sniffing, Abby nodded. Licking her lower lip, she tasted the salt of her own tears. "I—I found out that you've become very important to me, too."

His heart felt as if it had suspended its beat for a moment. Abby's face was damp with tears, and Alec ached to kiss them away. His hand tightened around hers. "What we have is special," he agreed huskily.

Rallying, Abby forced a smile. "We have another week together, and I think that's wonderful."

"I'm looking forward to it." Alec knew that if he continued to hold Abby's hand, he would kiss her. As much as he wanted to, he didn't dare because he didn't know if he could be satisfied with just a kiss. "I talked to Tim earlier, while you were sleeping. Oprah Winfrey wants us, and so does Phil Donahue. Apparently, for *Donahue* they are bringing Dr. Turner on to present an opposing viewpoint."

Groaning, Abby said, "You're kidding!"

"No. Tim wasn't too happy about it, either, but he pointed out that national exposure is more important for the whale issue than declining the invitation to appear on the show."

"That's going to be a rough time," Abby muttered.

"But it will also be an interesting show to do," Alec speculated. And then, his mouth curved into a thoughtful smile. "With your fiery belief and passion, the audience can't help but be won over by your love and commitment to the whales and dolphins. Don't worry, it will come out fine.''

Getting to her feet, Abby cast him a dubious look. ''I never thought Soviets were idealists, but you are one, Alec. Turner will try and gut me on national television. No, it's going to be a really visceral show, believe me.''

''I'll be there, if that helps.''

Abby turned toward him. ''You'll never know how much,'' she whispered.

Chapter Seven

"Let's show our viewers some photos of whales being harpooned and dolphins losing their lives in driftnets," Phil Donahue said.

Abby sat in the center of the dais of the immensely popular talk show. On her right was Alec in his Soviet officer's uniform, and on her left, Dr. Monica Turner. The lights were making Abby sweat. She hoped that her conservative gray suit and emerald-green silk blouse would make her look cool and calm, even though she wasn't. The horrifying pictures were flashed, one after another, and Abby tried to relax. It was impossible.

Dr. Monica Turner, a slender woman of fifty, with carefully coiffed blond hair, snorted as the slides were shown. She wore an off-white suit and a ruby-colored blouse. Her long fingernails were painted bright red. Abby thought the long fingernails were appropriate symbolically because Monica Turner was an adroit infighter, someone who didn't allow any threat to her post or reputation.

The audience's reaction was immediate. Abby heard the groans and outraged gasps. Next, Donahue ran the Soviet navy film of Abby's rescue by Alec, and then some short clips of their most recent showdown with the Japanese fleet in the Bering Sea.

Phil Donahue grimaced after the pictures had been shown. "Dr. Turner, what do you think about all this?" he asked, scratching his prematurely white hair.

"I think it's a bunch of activist hype, deliberately staged just to get the attention of shows like yours."

Abby forced herself not to move one facial muscle. She knew from Tim Atkin prepping her for this showdown that if she came off immature or overreactive to the audience, it would hurt the whale and dolphin issues.

Donahue cocked his head. "Dr. Fielding, what do think about Dr. Turner's opinion?"

"I don't consider saving whales or dolphins any less important than saving any other part of our environment from people who want to destroy it." Tim had told her not to engage Dr. Turner in an argument, so she stuck to the issue, the real issue, at hand.

"Interesting. Captain Rostov, is this Hollywood at sea, or do you consider the whale activists efforts legitimate?"

"Mr. Donahue, I can't comment on the politics of the SOWF. However, the Soviet Union has signed agreements promising to not only stop hunting the humpback and minke whales, which are on the border of extinction, but to present a united front to those countries who continued to flout a worldwide ban to save these mammals.''

"Don't you think SOWF is Hollywoodizing the whale's plight?'' Dr. Turner drawled, leaning over and buttonholing Alec with a disbelieving stare.

Alec smiled slightly. "Dr. Turner, in my country, *perestroika* has begun to encourage peaceful change rather than violence. I personally see the whale effort as a peaceful way to disagree.''

Monica glared at him. "It's highly unpeaceful! You call Dr. Fielding putting herself in that Zodiac and in the path of a catcher ship peaceful? I call it a flagrant violation of that Japanese whaler's rights on open and international seas!''

"It was a member of the same Japanese fleet that rammed the *Argonaut,* Dr. Turner,'' Alec reminded her. "Was what he was doing that time peaceful in your estimation?''

The audience tittered and Donahue gave a boyish smile as he came down the aisle, microphone in hand.

"How would you handle such a situation, Dr. Turner?'' Donahue asked, standing in front, one hand placed against his hip.

"If someone was stopping me from my livelihood,'' Monica snapped, "I'd feel I had the right to run over them!'' And then, belligerently, "The

SOWF is nothing but a liberal zealot organization comprised of old hippies from the sixties.''

Abby colored fiercely, clamped down on her retort and scrambled for a more diplomatic answer. Before she could, Alec spoke up.

"Dr. Turner, I've done a great deal of reading about America over the years. Isn't it true that your Native American people have a great respect for the environment? That they never fully harvest or destroy any plant or animal because they recognize they must live in harmony with it? I have always wondered why their philosophy, which to me is a sane middle road to tread, hasn't been explored or at least looked at by the American government with any degree of serious commitment. The SOWF, from what I read, follows a similar philosophical ideal that it's fine to harvest but necessary to leave enough behind so that a species may continue to reproduce and flourish. I think they, and people like Dr. Fielding, are trying to get the countries of the world to realize this wisdom in regards to the humpback and minke whales. Why not leave enough behind of these particular whales to proliferate so that they'll always be a part of our world ecology instead of obliterating them?''

Abby glanced at Monica. She had flushed a dull red, her eyes narrowed with anger. At that moment, Abby wanted to throw her arms around Alec and kiss him.

Sputtering, Monica leaned forward, both hands like claws on her chair. "Captain Rostov, your reading has obviously been one-sided. Our government doesn't want to see our environment ruined. We've poured millions of dollars into the EPA for hazardous materials cleanup in this country. We're committed."

"Then why hasn't President Reagan actively invoked the Pelly and Magnuson Amendments through your department, Dr. Turner?" Abby demanded coolly. "Those two laws say that the U.S. is able to place economic sanctions against countries who insist upon hunting endangered whale species. If the president is such an environmentalist, I should think he'd have enforced these laws to save the whales and dolphins. It's obvious to me that we're more interested in our economic relations with those countries that break the law than in protecting the mammals."

"Dr. Fielding," Monica said, "I feel that our economic security in the world is far more important than a few animal's problems. I would rather address the possible extinction of the human species than some lowly animal species."

Anger flooded Abby. "Dr. Turner, I view every living thing as being equally important. Whale and dolphin killing is a microcosm of a much larger problem. If we can't respect the gifts of this planet, both plant and animal, we won't be able to respect the lives of our fellow human beings, either.

"I find a lack of respect for every living thing on our planet right now," she continued. "Lack of respect for our elderly. Lack of respect for our children growing up without help and badly needed parental direction. The whale and dolphin issue simply mirrors, on a much smaller level, problems that also plague human beings."

"It's obvious that you're unable to address the issue before us," Monica said tightly. "You cannot compare whales and dolphins to human beings!"

"I think," Alec said, "if I may interrupt, that Dr. Fielding is trying to say that all living things deserve not only care, but respect. The Native Americans saw themselves as stewards of the Earth instead of owning or dominating all things. I believe if a stewardship approach were taken, that perhaps both people and animals would benefit tremendously."

Shaky with anger, Abby nodded. Alec's cool and calm approach was a decided advantage to the confrontation between her and Monica. "Regardless of what Dr. Turner thinks of the SOWF, we feel we are stewards to all living things," Abby whispered. Just as soon as possible, Abby was going to thank Alec for his wise input and ability to cut to the bone of the issue.

"Hold on!" Donahue called, and stretched out across several people to a women who stood up in the audience to voice her opinion.

"I think the environmental abuse in this country is appalling," the woman said. "How can we even think we can save other species of animals, if we can't even save ourselves from our own self-destruction?''

The audience clapped.

Dr. Turner laughed. "I think the issue is overstated. We're talking about two, out of many whale species, that are endangered."

Donahue ran all the way up the aisle to the rear of the audience. A man in a casual short-sleeved plaid shirt and jeans stood up. He gripped the microphone.

"Frankly, I think Dr. Turner has her priorities straight. Anytime some activist group grabs the headlines, all of America overreacts and goes to the extremes to try and correct the situation."

Donahue turned and went across the aisle to a small, petite woman in her thirties.

"Yeah! I say that human beings count first!"

Abby frowned. "Phil, that's exactly what's happened here in our country. Human need and greed has trampled, taken and stolen from every source of our planet. We need to learn to balance out our needs against our wants."

Donahue walked back down the aisle and rubbed his jaw. He looked over at Alec. "Captain Rostov, what do you think of all this?" He gestured broadly toward the audience.

"I think it's a good thing that Americans can safely speak their opinions without consequences from their government. But, I feel as Dr. Fielding does about our planet. We're becoming a global community, no longer cut off from one another. There is scientific evidence of worldwide deterioration in all spheres of our life, including our air, water and soil. It's fine to disagree, but I feel Americans are too selfish.''

''Selfish?'' Donahue's white eyebrows shot up. ''Would you care to elaborate?''

Alec opened his hands in a gesture of peaceful intent. ''In the past few weeks, I've been privileged to be in America. Never have I seen such richness and plenty. I also see Americans take for granted what they have. In the Soviet Union, our way of life is meager in comparison, our people always having to make concessions. Why use plastic containers when paper is biodegradable? Why use so many cars that foul the air when a train system is a cleaner mode of transportation? There are so many little ways that Americans could make concessions and still have their way of life. I don't understand why they don't see this, and I can only assume that they selfishly hoard their way of life because they are afraid of change for fear of losing it all.''

''Interesting,'' Donahue said, reflecting upon the idea.

Abby saw the faces of the audience, realizing Alec's statement had a terrific impact. Some people disagreed, and many others were silently nodding their heads. She applauded his courage to speak his truth.

"I don't think you've been in America long enough to speak with that kind of authority," Dr. Turner said.

Alec shrugged. "It was merely my observation and personal opinion, Dr. Turner. In the Soviet Union we have a saying, 'A dog doesn't foul it's own house.' I feel Americans are fouling their own country, the place where they must live, and it's not a good thing. Poisons, no matter what kind, catch up with one sooner or later. The whale and dolphin issue is symbolic of a much larger, global problem—respect of ourselves and all living things. We should try to work together and solve these problems, not annihilate species or habitat."

The audience burst into a thunderous roll of applause. Abby felt the tension drain from her as people cheered Alec's statement. Monica Turner was frowning, as usual.

Glancing at her watch, Abby realized in another half hour, the show would be over and they'd be going home. *Home.* The word sounded so good to Abby. Right now, what she needed was some peace and quiet—with Alec.

ON BOARD THEIR FLIGHT FOR Washington, D.C., Abby finally relaxed. Alec sat to her left, dressed in civilian attire. On her right was Tim Atkin, who was in uniform. The appearance on *Donahue* had been an intense hour of roller-coaster emotions for her. She hadn't had a moment's time alone with Alec since then, surrounded and hounded by reporters and television news people. Closing her eyes, she felt Alec's hand on hers.

"You should be proud, Abby. The audience were on your side."

She barely opened her eyes and squeezed his hand. "No small thanks to you. I was coming unglued. Every time Turner and I get in the same room, it's like fire and gasoline together."

Tim grinned. "Alec, you definitely saved the day. That Native American approach was dynamite! The audience really went for it. I was impressed."

"It was excellent," Abby agreed tiredly. "And just the right idea before I got up and ripped Monica Turner's heart out of her body."

Laughing, Alec patted her hand. "You wouldn't have done that."

"No, but the urge was there, believe me. I can't stand these politicos from the Hill that faithfully recite administration rhetoric. That's all it is. I can't stand it!"

"For the next four days, you've got Alec all to yourself," Tim teased. "Except for all the interviews that are going to spin off as a consequence of the two talk shows."

"Sure," Abby groaned, "our privacy is shot to ribbons."

"I might have a way to get you away from the hounding press the last night you're with us, Alec," Tim suggested.

Abby saw the glint in his eyes. "Okay, Tim, you're up to something again, as usual. What is it?"

His smile broadened. "You wanted me to meet your friend Susan for dinner at your apartment tomorrow night, right?"

"Right."

"Well, the *Eagle,* the Coast Guard Academy's tall ship, is in town for some official events. It's anchored at a pier in the Potomac. If Susan and I hit it off tomorrow night, I could wrangle a dinner invitation aboard the *Eagle* as an excuse for a second date with her. Besides, it would give Alec a chance to see a beautiful ship and have a nice place for you two to be alone for a while afterward."

"That's a great idea for a quiet dinner, *and,*" Abby emphasized, "a second date with Susan."

"If," Tim countered, "things work out between us. The idea popped into my head because I was looking for a way for you two to enjoy your last evening together—with privacy."

Abby was grateful. "Thanks, Tim."

Her heart contracted at the thought of Alec having to leave. Alec's hand was still on hers, and it felt good and right. In four days, she was going to lose his calm, steadying presence, his laughter and most of all, his sense of dry humor.

ALEC STOOD BACK, ADMIRING the crystal-and-china place settings on the table at Abby's apartment near Washington. Her second home was as large as her

Alaskan apartment and just as intimate. The carpet was wall-to-wall and a dusky-rose color. The drapes were pale pink and the furniture was brightly colored with flower designs. The dining area was a part of the kitchen, not really formal at all, Abby assured him. She was like a flighty bird moving between the stove and the table, wanting to make everything look just right for Susan and Tim's forthcoming first meeting.

Tim had arrived minutes earlier dressed in a conservative gray business suit. Alec wondered if he should have dressed more formally for the occasion, but Abby shook her head. He looked so handsome in his new jeans. Abby was in a pair of dark green slacks, a mint green blouse set off with a multicolored scarf. On her, Alec thought the outfit looked stunning. Her hair was held back in what looked like a horse's mane and he liked the effect because it made Abby look wild and free, which was her nature.

When the doorbell rang, Abby answered the door. Both men were standing in the living area, wineglasses in hand, their focus immediate. Abby's heart speeded up. She knew Susan was reluctantly coming to dinner to meet Tim, and doing it only because Abby had begged her to come.

"Hi," Abby greeted Susan and Courtney breathlessly as she opened the door. Susan, who stood five-feet six-inches tall, smiled nervously. She wore a long light wool skirt of dark brown set off with an ivory blouse with a green and gold scarf at the throat.

"Hi, yourself. I'm sorry we're a little late," Susan apologized, smiling down at Courtney. "But a girl likes to take her time with a new dress, you know."

Abby leaned down and hugged Courtney, who willingly came from behind her mother's long brown skirt. "You look beautiful in your new pink dress! How pretty you look, sweetheart." She kissed Courtney's cheek. The girl had dark brown hair and blue eyes just like her mother's. Abby was always amazed at how much they resembled each other. Susan had braided her daughter's thin hair into two small pigtails that were tied off with Cookie Monster barrettes.

"Hi, Aunt Abby," Courtney said shyly. She held up her favorite stuffed toy. "Look, I got Wendy the Whale with me."

Abby grinned. She'd bought Wendy for Courtney last year when she was at Sea World for vacation in San Diego. "Why, Wendy looks so happy to be with you. Do you still sleep with her every night?"

Susan nodded. "Sure does. And just like you promised, Wendy keeps the bad dreams away from her."

Touched, Abby led them into the living room. She saw how terribly awkward Susan really was around men. Putting on a brave front, Susan nervously smiled and shook hands with Tim, who was the epitome of a gentleman. It was obvious that Tim liked Susan very much. Worried, Abby watched Courtney, who was hiding behind her mother's skirt watching Tim and Alec through wary eyes.

"Honey," Susan whispered, placing her hand on her daughter's pigtailed hair, "I want you to meet Lieutenant Tim Atkin from the Coast Guard." Susan gave Tim a look that spoke volumes, that said she hoped he understood her daughter's painful shyness.

Tim crouched down and gave her a warm smile. A few feet away, Courtney held her mother's skirt in both her small fists, hiding behind it. "Hiya, Squirt. Hey, you know when I found out you liked animals from the sea, I thought you might like this." He pulled a small stuffed toy from the pocket of his suit coat. "This is Wally the Whale, Wendy's mate." He slowly offered the toy to Courtney. "When Abby told me about Wendy, I figured you might like to have Wally, too."

Courtney's eyes widened. She looked up at her mother.

Susan laughed delightedly. "Go ahead, honey."

One small hand released Susan's skirt and reached up to the toy. Her tiny fingers wrapped gently around Wally. The instant she had the stuffed toy, she quickly stepped back behind her mother for safety.

Tim grinned and stood up, his gaze on Susan. "She's a beautiful little girl. You must be very proud of her."

Blushing, Susan hugged her daughter. "Courtney's very special to me. I just don't have the time to spend with her I'd like, though."

Tim nodded, understanding. "Quality time with anyone is everyone's problem these days," he agreed.

Thrilled that Courtney accepted the gift from Tim, Abby turned away. She quickly wiped the tears from her eyes. Tim didn't realize how much the little girl trusted him to do what she'd just done. But Susan did, because her eyes were misty looking, too. As Abby went into the kitchen, she hoped Susan realized just how special a man Tim Atkin really was.

Alec quietly approached Abby. He placed his hand on her shoulder as she busied herself with carving the yankee pot roast. Although she was vegetarian, she didn't expect her friends to eat her kind of food, so had prepared a meat meal for them.

"Are you all right?" he asked, bending over to look at her.

"Sure...." Abby sniffed. "It's just that Susan and Courtney have gone through so much. I didn't know what to expect from Courtney when she was introduced to Tim. Usually, she cries and wants to go home."

"She didn't with me the other day when you introduced us," Alec said gently, massaging her tense shoulders and neck.

Abby smiled up at him through a wall of tears. "No, but then, you're special, too. A wounded animal, or a wounded human being can unconsciously sense when someone is kind and gentle. You and Tim are like that, you know.''

"I'll settle for being special in your eyes," Alec whispered, and he turned her around so that he could wipe the last traces of her tears away from her cheeks with his thumbs. "There."

Being in the circle of Alec's arms was the most natural thing in the world to Abby. His sensitivity to her, to everyone, was incredible.

Wiping her hands on the dishcloth, Abby whispered, "Will you help me put the food on the table?"

"Of course." Alec glanced over his shoulder and looked into the living room. "Ah, good. Tim and Susan are sitting on the couch together. He just poured her some wine."

Abby reached up and embraced Alec. She gave him a brief hug. "And you accuse *me* of matchmaking. You're just as bad as I am, Captain Rostov!"

"Guilty as charged," he chuckled, hugging her back, wanting more, much more, but knowing now was not the time or place.

"OH, ABBY, THE POT ROAST was delicious. I'm stuffed like the proverbial turkey," Susan sighed. She smiled at her daughter, who had also cleaned up her plate. Courtney had both her pet whales on the table next to her.

Tim patted his stomach, having taken off his suit coat a long time ago, his shirt sleeves rolled up to just below his elbows and the collar of his shirt opened at the throat, minus the tie. "I'll second that. Hey, Squirt, I bet Wally and Wendy are stuffed up to their gills. What do you think?"

Courtney's eyebrows rose and she craned her neck to closely study her toy friends. "Dunno," she muttered.

"You might press on their tummies and see," Tim suggested.

Susan's eyes mirrored disbelief when her daughter did exactly as Tim suggested. She looked over at the Coast Guard officer as if to silently ask what kind of magic he wielded with her daughter. Tim smiled shyly.

"I'm the youngest of a family of five children," he explained to Susan, reading the question in her eyes. "I've got two older brothers in the Coast Guard, and my father was a navy pilot for twenty-five years before that. I remember all the tricks they played on me to get me to do something when I didn't want to do it."

Abby laughed softly. She watched as Courtney lifted her chin and studied Tim critically. There was something about the Coast Guard officer that imbued her with trust, if only a little bit. Glancing at Susan, Abby saw gratefulness and something else mirrored in her best friend's eyes. Abby liked what she saw in them and happily stood up.

"Everyone except Alec out of the kitchen! I'm serving cherry pie with vanilla ice cream in the living room. Coffee for the adults, and milk for Courtney!"

Tim got up, quickly moved to Susan's chair and pulled it out for her.

"Why...thank you."

"Chivalry," Tim told her in a conspiratorial tone, "didn't die in the Coast Guard like it did everywhere else when feminism came in."

Blushing, Susan murmured, "Nobody has ever done this for me." And then she laughed softly. "You're spoiling me, Tim."

Before Abby could warn Tim, he stepped around to Courtney's chair.

"May I help you, Wendy and Wally away from the table?" Tim asked. "You know, they teach us academy graduates to always mind our manners, that we're supposed to help ladies—and whales—away from the table after dinner. May I?"

Courtney nodded, picked up her two friends and allowed Tim to pull the chair away from the table. She slid off and walked over to her mother.

"Amazing," Susan said, looking over at Tim in complete awe.

"But wonderful," Abby whispered, thrilled with Courtney's acceptance of Tim. "Shoo! All of you, out of the kitchen! Alec, cut the pie for me while I clear dishes?"

"Of course."

The kitchen quieted in a few moments. Alec dutifully cut thick portions of the pie and then added the vanilla ice cream to the top of each one. Abby was rinsing the dishes and placing them in the dishwasher.

"Did you see Susan's face when Tim helped her from the table?" Abby asked. "She was about ready to drop over in a faint!"

"I saw other things in her eyes, too," Alec told her in a conspiratorial tone.

With a grin, Abby whispered, "Do you think there's hope for them?"

Picking up the plates, Alec nodded. "Like Siskel and Ebert, I'll give their budding relationship two thumbs-up."

Laughing, Abby followed Alec into the living room with dessert in hand. He'd gotten a chance to watch some television the other evening, and the movie reviewers, Siskel and Ebert, had been enthusiastically giving their opinions on newly released films. He also liked *Entertainment Tonight,* and faithfully recited to Abby that Tom Cruise was getting married to Mimi Rogers, and that Rita Hayworth, a great actress, had died. Alec caught on fast to Americana, Abby decided warmly.

As she entered the living room, Abby's delight multiplied. Courtney was sitting at the coffee table opposite of the couch where Tim and Susan sat. The little girl kept looking at Tim, studying him for long moments at a time, a perplexed but curious look on her small oval features. Abby took that as a positive sign.

"Hey," Tim called out to them, "Courtney's decided she, Wendy and Wally want to go on board the *Eagle* with us, four days from now for our farewell dinner with Alec. How about that?"

"Wonderful!" Abby said, handing them the pie. Just the thought that Alec's last night in the U.S. wasn't faraway, saddened Abby to a degree she never thought possible. What would her world be like without his presence? Hollow and empty. Trying to put her personal feelings aside for the sake of her company, Abby forced a brave smile and sat with Courtney at the coffee table.

"Miss Manners wouldn't approve," Susan chided her with a laugh.

"No," Abby laughed, "Miss Manners wouldn't want to come into my apartment for dinner. I'm sure she'd have a hemorrhage if she saw us eating dessert from a coffee table while we sat on the floor."

"This is family living and eating," Tim said. "Nothing wrong with having dessert on the coffee table, is there, Squirt?"

All eyes focused on Courtney. She looked up solemnly at Tim. "Wendy and Wally like it."

"Then," Tim whispered, leaning over with his napkin and removing a speck of ice cream from the corner of Courtney's mouth, "that's all that counts, isn't it?"

Susan shook her head. She glanced over at Abby. "Can you believe this?" she asked her.

With a sigh, Abby smiled at Tim. "I told you he was a very special person. Now, maybe you'll believe me." Courtney never allowed a stranger to touch her. Yet when Tim had leaned over and cleaned off her mouth, Courtney accepted his touch as if it were the most natural thing in the world between them. Glancing at Alec, who sat in one of the two maple rockers, she saw the warmth and compassion dancing in his eyes.

Her heart was filled with happiness. Abby sat cross-legged on the floor and enjoyed her friends. There wasn't much more in the world she could wish for, except that Alec wouldn't have to leave. Their world would come to an end shortly. After the planned meal aboard the *Eagle,* he'd be flown to the airport—and would be gone forever from her life.

Chapter Eight

"The *Eagle* is beautiful ship," Alec told Abby in a hushed tone as they walked arm in arm around the shadowy deck. He raised his head, admiring the many masts of the ship, the web of ropes hanging from them holding the furled canvas sheets captive. Dinner in the wardroom had been a lively and engaging experience. Below, on the pier, Tim walked Susan and Courtney back to the parking lot. Susan would drive home, and Tim would drive Abby and Alec to the waiting helicopter that would take Alec to the airport.

"The night is beautiful," Abby whispered as she leaned out over the highly polished brass railing to look at the placid waters of the Potomac. It was nearly 11:00 p.m., and there was a peaceful silence that blanketed the river and the pier area. Lights suspended from the masts shed a soft light across the deck of the ship, providing just enough illumination to see where one walked, but allowing two people, if they wanted, to hide in the embrace of the darkness. Tonight, Abby did.

Her voice had wobbled. Had Alec heard the emotion she was trying so hard to keep at bay?

He moved alongside her, his hand near hers on the rail. "You barely ate anything tonight, Abby."

"I know...."

"I didn't, either." With a shrug, he added in a strained voice, "I don't want to have to leave you."

Abby turned and looked up into his serious features etched out of darkness and light. "You're so unlike American men. They'd play a game with me, but you don't. You go straight to the heart of the matter."

Lifting his hand, he caressed her cheek. "When one's heart is involved, there can be no games," Alec whispered. Her flesh was firm and velvet beneath each stroke of his thumb. He saw her eyes grow soft, and the longing grew tenfold within him. How many times in these last three weeks had Alec wanted to kiss her? He'd lost count.

Closing her eyes, Abby nuzzled against Alec's hand. "I'm going to miss you more than I ever thought possible."

With a groan, Alec pulled her into his arms. As Abby melted against him, he sighed. Her arms went around his waist and she clung to him. "*Moya edinstvenaya,* my only one."

Burying her face against his shoulder and neck, Abby tried to fight the flow of tears that wanted to come, but she couldn't. "The time with you," she whispered, her voice cracking, "has been like a dream, Alec. A beautiful dream. And it's coming to an end tonight." At 1:00 a.m., a Soviet airliner would take off from Kennedy Airport. After one last press conference, Alec would leave—forever.

Gently threading his fingers through her loose, glorious hair, Alec felt the silken strength of the strands. The spicy perfume Abby wore made him heady, made him want to forget about going back to the Soviet Union. "I understand." His voice was none too steady, either. Abby felt heavenly in his arms. Alec was hotly aware of the way her body curved, met and touched his.

"One of my favorite poets, Evgeny Baratynsky, who lived in the early 1800s, wrote something I think applies to us," he told her quietly. "It is called 'Love' and he says, 'In love we drink the sweet poison; / and yet we drink it, / And pay for the brief joy / With the unhappiness of many days. / The fire of love is the fire of life, / they say; but what is it that we see? / It empties and destroys / The soul it embraces. / But who, o love, can stifle the memories / Of your splendid days? / Then I would come to life again to taste of joy, / To dream the golden dreams of blooming youth, / To open again my soul to you.'"

Abby sniffed and lifted her head. Alec's eyes burned with such heat for her alone, that she trembled. As he placed his fingers beneath her chin, a soft sigh issued from her lips. Never had she wanted to kiss a man more, never had she wanted to know a man better.

"I would drink the sweet poison of your lips, Abby, and share my brief joy at being with you. . . ."

As he leaned down, his eyes narrowed upon her, Abby leaned upward, her arms tightening around Alec. "No regrets," she whispered achingly.

"No," he rasped, "no regrets . . ."

His mouth fitted perfectly against hers, and heat swept through her like a bolt of lightning. She tasted the coffee, the chocolate dessert on his lips, and hungrily returned his fiery need of her. Suddenly, the world ceased to exist as Abby lost herself in the taste, texture and senses of Alec as a man. A man of incomparable strength and gentleness, as his mouth nipped and cajoled her to glory in their union.

Slowly, ever so slowly, Alec disengaged. It was the last thing in the world he wanted to do. Abby's eyes were dazed and lustrous after the branding, burning kiss. She swayed against him, and he fitted his hand against her hip to steady her. He was dizzy himself. Dizzy with the knowledge and intoxication of her fiery response.

"You are as hot as the color of your hair," he rasped, briefly touching the long, shining strands across her shoulder. The ache to lean down, to sweep Abby uncompromisingly into his arms and love her was pulverizing him internally. As she lifted her eyelashes, her mouth wet and parted from his kiss, Alec groaned softly. "You are a woman of fire, *moya edinstvenaya. My* woman of fire...."

Alec placed his hand around her waist, drew her close and began the walk slowly across the deck. There were no words Abby could say because she was snared in a web of molten heat that flowed through every vibrating cell in her body. As they walked down the gangplank to the pier below and then toward the parking lot, where Tim stood waiting for them, Abby tried to gather her escaping emotions.

Once in the car, grateful for the darkness cloaking her, she hoped that Tim wouldn't see the devastation she was sure was written on her face. Alec's arm around her gave her solace, but not comfort. Abby leaned against Alec, her face buried beneath his jaw.

"I've given you my address," he told her quietly. "I will write, Abby."

"I'm a lousy letter writer," she said, "but you'll hear from me. That's a promise."

He smiled faintly, the pain around his heart nearly too much to bear. "I will always think of Baratynsky's poem with new awareness," he told her wryly.

"I'll never forget it," Abby said, sitting up. She turned and placed her hand against his cheek. The prickly feeling of his beard reminded her that he always got a five o'clock shadow. In the changing light, he looked dangerous in all ways to her wildly beating heart.

"When I get back aboard the *Udaloy,* I'll write the poem down and send it to you. Russian poets always speak from their heart and soul."

Abby felt as if her soul were being ripped apart. Words were so useless right now. "I've learned so much about the Soviet Union through you, Alec. Good things. Wonderful things."

He smiled sadly and pressed her hand against his cheek. "America is no longer some dark, threatening place I was raised to believe that it was." He leaned over and kissed her lips gently. "I will remember the woman with the courage to challenge the world because of her passionate belief that all things deserve to live in harmony with one another."

Abby forced back a sob. She didn't want Alec's last picture of her to be one of tears. Later, she could cry out the loss of him in her life at home, in the privacy of her apartment.

"We're here," Tim called over his shoulder.

Abby looked out the front window of the vehicle. There, on a landing pad, was the H-65, a white Coast Guard helicopter with the international red-orange stripe on its tail. She felt Alec's hand tighten around hers.

"You could fly with me to the airport. It would give us a few more minutes together."

She shook her head and looked away, fighting to not cry. "N-no, it's better this way, Alec. I'm lousy at goodbyes." She forced herself to look up at him, his face imprinted forever on the memory of her aching heart. She smoothed the fabric of his dark blue uniform, then she rested her hand against his chest. "I'd get your uniform all wet. You're going to a news conference. You need to look your best, not have dark splotches of tears all over your jacket."

He smiled and looked down at his uniform. There were already several small damp spots left by the tears she was trying so hard not to release right now. He pressed his hand across them. "These are like medals. I'll wear them proudly and without apology in front of the whole world, Abby." He brushed away a tear clinging to her lashes. "Tears are the gateway to the soul, didn't you know that?"

It took everything Abby had not to burst into a torrent of sobs. She sat there holding herself stiffly, not even daring to breathe for that moment because his words unstrung her like nothing else ever could. Finally, she choked out, "Goodbye, Alec."

"Farewell, *moya edinstvenaya,*" he breathed, leaning down, kissing her one last time, a kiss that had to last forever.

Abby tore her mouth away from his as she drowned in the splendor of his unchecked fire, the beauty of him as a consummate man, sensitive and caring. She sat there as Alec left his seat and climbed out of the car. Tears blurred Abby's vision, warm streams running down her cheeks. She wasn't going to be able to hold back her tears until she got home, the pain, the loss, were too great.

Tim shook Alec's hand, the warmth between the two men obvious, and escorted him to the helicopter. Unable to watch Alec walk to the awaiting aircraft, Abby sat back in the seat. She heard the whine of the helicopter engine and then the whooshing sound of the rotor as it began to move faster and faster.

Finally, the aircraft engine revved up to a high whine, and Abby knew the helicopter was going to take off. She wiped her eyes with her trembling fingers and watched the Coast Guard aircraft slowly lift off the pad and become swallowed up in the darkness of the night. Only the blinking red and green lights showed where the helicopter was in the fabric of the night sky. Sniffing, Abby hunted for and found a tissue in her purse. After wiping her eyes, she got out and moved into the front seat beside Tim.

Tim took off his cap and placed it on the rear seat. "How are you doing?" he asked quietly, studying her gravely.

"Rotten," Abby whispered.

"You're really one brave lady, you know that?"

Abby shook her head. The car started forward, and she leaned back, the tissue pressed to her eyes. "I don't feel very brave right now, Tim. I feel like hell."

His mouth tightened. "I'm sorry, Abby. For both of you. To me, it was obvious from the first moment I met Alec that there was something special you two had going for you."

Sniffing, Abby nodded. "I—I just feel like someone's ripped out my heart. I've never had this feeling before. It's awful."

The lights along the thoroughfare blipped through the car window, cascading them alternately with brightness and then darkness. "As I was walking back from the helo, I was trying to put myself in your place. I've just met Susan and Courtney. What would it be like to know that I had to walk out of their lives forever after just meeting them, liking them . . . ?"

Abby lifted her head and looked over at Tim's grim profile. "You like Susan that much?"

He glanced over at her. "That much. Keep it a secret, though. Susan's really been hurt, and she's gun-shy of me. I want to go real slow with her. Maybe, with time, she'll trust me as much as Courtney does." He smiled a little.

Despite her own agony, Abby reached out and gripped Tim's arm. "This is wonderful," she whispered unsteadily. "I was so hoping that you'd like one another."

"Like?" Tim said. "More like being knocked alongside the head with a two-by-four, Abby."

Her mouth dropped open. "Really?"

"Really. I can't get her out of my thoughts. I lay awake at night thinking about Susan. I go around during the day thinking about her. When I do sleep, I dream about her." He shook his head. "I know we're a generation that has lost its ability to be romantic and idealistic because of so much going down but, Abby, I feel all those things when I'm with Susan."

Sitting back in the seat, Abby said nothing. The pain in her heart over Alec's leaving was no less, but at least now a ribbon of joy shared that spot in her breast. "Oh, Tim, I hope that things work out between you and Susan. She deserves someone like you after all the hell she's gone through. And so does Courtney."

He laughed, a little shy after his admission. "Her deserve me? Hell, I'm wondering what I did to deserve someone like her!"

Patting her shoulder, Abby said, "Just persevere, Tim. Susan needs your patience and understanding."

"I know that. I sense it."

"Funny," Abby said softly, "how much you and Alec are alike, do you know that? Men are finally starting to understand and embrace the idea that being sensitive, being able to show feelings and even cry aren't signs of weakness. They're signs of strength. That's what women need—men who aren't afraid of those feelings and emotions. Men like you."

"Well," Tim said, giving her a game smile, "we're trying, Abby. But it's tough on us, too. We've been molded and stamped into pushing away what we felt. Society hasn't done men or women any favors as far as I'm concerned. I think it's fine that women expect more from us, but I also feel that they need to allow us that room to grow, too.''

"This decade's been hard on everybody," Abby agreed. "People seem more interested in instant gratification, money, labels and careers than some of the more important things."

"Yeah, like family, honor, values and morals, just to name a few."

"You come from a military family where those things were important and stressed in your life," Abby said.

"Believe me, I consider myself lucky. I don't want to be like a lot of those people of our generation, Abby. We've lost the threads of family and what it means. Little Courtney's going to be a latch-key kid in a few more years. It hurts me to think that that will happen to her, to any child. I know a woman has to work right alongside her husband to make ends meet, but the children are falling through the cracks. They're paying for our race to get material possessions."

"There are no easy answers, Tim."

"Well," he said stubbornly, "if things go the way I want them to, Courtney won't be a latch-key kid. There's options. I know there are. If Susan and I can put our heads together, both of us make compromises, we can solve some of these problems. Maybe, if Susan falls head over heels for me like I have with her, we can make this work. It won't be easy, but I know it can be done. My parents have been married for forty years. I want the same kind of marriage.''

"Disposable marriages have been the rage," Abby agreed, thinking of Alec. "I wonder if people in the Soviet Union view marriage like we do?"

"I doubt it. Alec's old-fashioned, like me. Commitment means something to him. At the first sign of trouble, you don't jump ship and bail out."

"Susan's case was different, though," Abby pointed out gently.

Grimly, Tim nodded. "If I ever meet her ex-husband, I'm going to beat him to a bloody pulp. I swear I will."

"Makes two of us," Abby said. "He's the epitome of men at their worst."

"Which," Tim sighed, "is the problem I've got with Susan. Steve broke her trust with all men, and that includes myself. Until she can see me for me and not 'all men,' I won't get to first base with her."

"Time," Abby whispered. "With time, that will happen, Tim. I just feel it here, in my heart."

With a grateful smile, Tim muttered, "I hope you're right, Abby, because I've met the woman I want to marry. Now all I have to do is convince her."

"You will," she said softly. "I know you will, Tim."

"Look, I know you're hurting over Alec's leaving. If there's anything I can do to help, let me know, okay? I've got use of certain diplomatic channels, so I can make things happen up to a point."

Abby shook her head, tears welling up behind her eyelids once again. She was going to cry. Part of her tears was for Susan and the happiness she knew that Tim could bring to the relationship. The other part was for the loss of Alec to herself. Her heart felt raw, and she felt like a lone wolf wanting to howl at the moon because she'd lost her mate. She'd given advice to Tim—but could time help assuage her loss?

"ABBY, YOU LOOK AWFUL!" Susan said as she came into the apartment with Courtney.

Abby looked up from the breakfast bar where she sat, papers scattered all around her. "Oh...hi, Susan." She forced a smile. Courtney was holding both whales in one hand, a smile on her face. She wore a Muppet T-shirt with the Cookie Monster on it, and a well worn pair of jeans.

"Am I interrupting?" Susan halted midway into the living room.

"No, not at all! I haven't seen you in almost two weeks. Come on, let's sit down and talk. Gosh, I've been so busy—"

Susan went into the kitchen and poured them each a glass of wine. "Tell me about it. Are you working yourself into the ground? Last week it was the talk shows, this week the radio shows. Don't you ever stop?"

"The truth?" Tiredly, Abby slid off the stool, accepted the wine from her friend and joined her on the couch. Courtney played happily on the floor with her two whales near the coffee table.

"Nothing but." Susan folded her leg beneath her, dressed in a pair of pale peach slacks, a white blouse and peach blazer. She'd just gotten home from work, and it was 7:00 p.m.

Sipping the wine, Abby shrugged. "I miss Alec."

"No kidding. You've got awful circles under your eyes. Are you trying to forget him by working yourself into an early grave?"

Wasn't that the truth, Abby thought. "I—well, I just didn't realize how much he'd meant to me until he was gone, Susan." She looked around the apartment, her voice lowering with pain. "This place is so empty without his presence. You'd think I had a good dose of puppy love or something." Wrinkling her nose, Abby muttered, "Tim's right, our generation has lost a lot of things, among them, romance, idealism, hope...."

Reaching out, Susan gripped Abby's hand. "I can see the hurt in your eyes, and I'm sorry. Alec is a wonderful man, just like Tim is."

Sadly, Abby smiled and squeezed Susan's hand. "Many good things came out of meeting Alec. Donations totaling four million dollars have come in because of the shows we were on together. The SOWF people are ecstatic, and so am I. The money will go directly to the whale fund to create even more awareness through ads and radio spots. Just as important, you met Tim."

Susan sat back and released a deep sigh. "Tim . . . God, Abby, he's too good to be true. I've seen him every weekend for a couple of hours. I wish it were for a longer time, but my brokerage firm is really putting the pressure on me to get into junk bonds, and I'm doing my damndest not to. I'm spending a lot more time doing research for my investment-portfolio customers to diversify in other areas. It's a real uphill battle."

"I wish they'd let you do your thing."

"Yeah, me, too."

"So things are going smoothly between you and Tim?"

Susan squirmed.

"Well?" Abby baited, genuinely interested in her friend's escalating happiness.

Susan rubbed her brow. "He's a dream, Abby. I'm afraid to believe in him. Afraid to believe he's real. Tim's the opposite of Steve in every way possible. He's got a great sense of humor, he's gentle and not pushy." She shook her head. "Do you know that Tim has only kissed me twice in the month we've been seeing one another? And that's it!"

A smile tugged at Abby's mouth, some of the heaviness from around her heart lifting. It was so good to see the happiness in Susan's eyes. "You mean he hasn't jumped your bones like you expected?" she teased.

"Ouch, I had that coming, didn't I?"

"You're conditioned to it, Susan. Tim's old-fashioned. He may be from our generation, but he's got strong values."

"I like what he is," Susan admitted softly. "He's not trying to push me into bed with him or to manipulate me like other guys have in the past. It's such a different kind of relationship than I've had, and frankly, I'm on totally new ground with him. Sometimes, I don't know how to react to him. He just kind of gives me that boyish smile of his and steps back."

"Just keep trusting one another." Abby gestured toward her mass of paperwork on the counter. "In the meantime, I'm going to continue my whale-awareness campaign."

"Well," Susan said gently, "you're sure doing your part to uplift world consciousness." She reached over, barely touching Abby's drooped shoulder. "But you're killing yourself doing it."

"I'm trying to bury myself in work to not feel or think about Alec."

"I know. Have you heard from him lately?"

"I've gotten two letters from him . . . early on. Traveling so much, I haven't been able to write to him as much as I'd like. Tim was kind enough to send him a short message for me a couple of days ago." Abby sighed. "And now I've got to prepare a speech that I'll give at the U.N. next week."

Susan gave her an admiring look. "You're really becoming famous, Abby."

"I don't care one whit about fame. It's an empty vessel for me. I see it as a vehicle to be used to get the word out about our dying world."

"I know a lot of people who'd love to have the power that's been handed to you. Dr. Monica Turner, for one."

"Her." The word came out flat. Abby got up and began to pace. "She's stonewalling us on the Hill, Susan. The SOWF lobbyist has new legislation written and ready to go, but Turner's going behind closed doors of Congress and telling them that enough's been written into law. She's trying to get it killed in committee before it ever reaches a vote in the House. If we can't get this legislation accepted, it's...well...I don't know...."

"Abby, you can't take responsibility for it failing or being accepted. Look at you—you've lost weight. This has to stop."

Pressing her fingertips to her temples, Abby stood in the middle of the living room. "You're right, but I can't walk away from what was created, Susan. The public awareness has to be escalated. If Congress and the president refuse to help us, we've got to go to the people." She smiled tiredly. "There's one thing I love about the American people. Once they truly comprehend the depth of a problem, they'll rally and respond. That's why I'm doing all these radio and television talk shows to create that kind of awareness."

"Well, I'm worried for you."

"I'll be okay. Soon all the fanfare that was created a month ago will die down. The press will jump on the next disaster and the whales will be forgotten. It's the American way."

"Knowing you, you won't let the American people forget."

"No," Abby vowed huskily, "I won't. When Alec saved my life, I changed a lot, Susan. I really thought I was going to die. When I woke up and he was at my side, I realized how precious, how fragile life really is. I realized I can live for more than just the moment. I can live for now and build productively toward the future as I envision it. Someday, soon I hope, Americans will do the right thing."

Susan got up and came over to Abby. She placed her arm around her shoulders. "Listen, you're tired. Go take a hot bath and then go to bed, okay?"

Abby nodded. But she knew that when she slept— what little she slept—dreams of Alec, of what they'd shared, haunted her. Would there come a time when she wouldn't feel filled with so much promise of a future they'd never share?

Chapter Nine

Abby held herself in tight check as she tried to cultivate her short span of patience while in Dr. Monica Turner's outer office waiting to be summoned by the woman herself. As she sat, dressed in a pale pink business suit, Abby wondered what her archenemy from the State Department wanted from her.

Rubbing her aching temple, Abby continued to work on the speech she would deliver to the U.N. tomorrow at 10:00 a.m. Perhaps the prospect of her speech was giving Turner the jitters. Or maybe it was giving the administration a twinge. Good, they deserved it, in Abby's opinion. Yesterday, the SOWF lobbyist had been able to get in to see a very influential congressman about the proposed whale and dolphin legislation. Was that what had scared Turner out of hiding?

The buzzer on Pat Monahan's desk beeped. Abby saw the secretary nod in her direction, her face pinched with disapproval.

"Dr. Turner will now see you, Dr. Fielding."

Abby rose and picked up her scarred and scratched briefcase that was ten years old. "Thank you," she responded coolly. Her stomach was tight with tension, and Abby knew as she walked into the office that she had to keep her temper in check as never before. Alec had been right: her red hair was a warning to anyone that her temper was volatile. This morning, she could not afford to lose it.

The office was huge, and Abby halted in the middle of the Oriental rug and looked around. There were certificates, diplomas and a number of pictures of Dr. Turner with key administration officials tastefully arranged on the mahogany-paneled walls. Monica sat behind her rectangular maple desk, a pair of tortoiseshell-framed bifocals resting on her nose. She looked over them at Abby.

"Come in, Dr. Fielding." Monica gestured to a red leather wing chair that sat to one side of her desk. "Coffee?"

Surprised at the low, mellow tone of Monica's voice, Abby shook her head. "No, thank you."

"Oh, that's right. I read somewhere that you were a health-food addict."

"Better that kind of addict than the other types of addicts we have in this country, don't you think, Dr. Turner?"

Monica leaned back in her chair and glanced over at Pat, who stood poised at the door. "No disagreement from me. Bring us tea with lemon." She glanced at Abby as she sat down. "You do drink tea, don't you?"

"Herbal tea, if you have any. If not, a glass of ice water will do fine."

Monica smiled briefly. "Contrary to popular opinion, I am concerned with all kinds of health matters, Dr. Fielding." Directing her attention to her secretary, she said, "Two cups of chamomile tea, please."

Abby tried to appear relaxed and crossed her legs. She set her briefcase down beside the chair. "Chamomile. That's an herbal tea to soothe the nerves."

Monica sat up and removed her bifocal glasses, letting them hang around her neck on a gold chain. "Working around here is enough to put anyone's nerves on edge."

"No argument from me," Abby said dryly. Monica's blond hair was carefully coiffed in a chignon, giving her narrow face a severe look. But it was belied by the blue miniskirt she wore. Although miniskirts were suddenly the rage again, Abby noted that hardly any women in business wore them. They preferred conservative hemlines. If she didn't know Monica worked for the State Department, she'd have been an ideal magazine model.

Monica gave her a quick, bloodless smile and waited until her secretary had delivered the tea on a silver serving tray and then left. The door closed, and she gestured to Abby to help herself.

"Vitamin C in the form of lemon, chamomile for our collective nerves, and honey instead of sugar." She pinned Abby with a dark look. "You see, perhaps we're not so far apart as you'd like to think we are."

Abby got up and squeezed the lemon into the gold-colored tea. "This is a surprise, I'll admit that," she told the woman. "But on issues that are far larger and more weighty, it's a known fact we're polar opposites, Dr. Turner."

Monica took her cup and saucer and sat back in her overstuffed leather chair. She sipped the tea and remained silent for a moment. "You know, I'm envious of all the press that you've gotten this last month. But I also admire what you did."

Abby sipped the tea, not tasting it. Monica wasn't to be trusted under any circumstances, and Abby had the feeling the woman was trying to maneuver her. For what, Abby wasn't sure—yet. "Admire what I did? I don't understand."

"Oh," Monica whispered in her contralto voice, "I think you do. Come now, Dr. Fielding, we're alone now. We're not sitting on the front lines of *Donahue* any longer with a million viewers eavesdropping. You can admit the truth."

"Truth about what?"

"That you deliberately staged the collision with that poor, hapless Japanese whaling ship. And in doing so, it set up a perfect reason for you to be flung overboard in front of the rolling cameras."

Anger singed her tension. Abby smiled tightly, derision in her voice. "Oh, yes, and I just managed to snag the attention of a Soviet navy helicopter so it could photograph what had happened, as well as rescue me." Abby gave her a steely look. "Just between you and me, Dr. Turner, none of it was rigged."

"That's not the opinion of some higher-ups in the administration."

"I could care less what this administration thinks," Abby flared. "As far as I'm concerned, they've shown their callous disregard to all life forms in general in the last seven years!"

"Come now," Monica said smoothly, leaning back and enjoying her tea, "the Reagan years will go down in history as one of the best periods of the century."

"To whom? The rich? The corporations? Oh, I'm sure with them he's a real Hollywood hero. But ask the homeless and the elderly who have had so many programs cut out from under them. Sorry, but I'll wait a decade and then see how the man you work for is treated by the historians."

Chuckling, Monica said, "Dr. Fielding, one of the many fascinating things about you is your childlike fanaticism and your oversimplification of problems in general." She looked at Abby with one eyebrow raised. "I really don't know how you got a doctorate in marine biology when you're so unscientific and illogical."

Abby sat there controlling her volatile temper. She knew Monica Turner was deliberately trying to provoke her. Setting down the teacup, Abby gritted out, "Let's cut to the chase. Why did you want to see me?"

Still smiling, Monica sipped her tea, quiet settling into the office once again. "As I said, I've admired how much press and attention you've squeezed out of your Bering Sea experience. And I'm even more surprised that the U.N. is allowing you to speak to them as a body."

That was it, Abby decided. Dr. Turner was worried about her U.N. speech. "Fortunately, other people see the simplicity of what's going on with the whales and dolphins like I do. The members of the U.N. invited me to speak. I didn't go pounding on their door begging for an opportunity to give this speech."

"I see...." With a small frown, Monica put her tea aside and placed her elbows on the desk. "The administration is very interested in what you're going to say, Dr. Fielding. Might you share that with me?"

Satisfaction thrummed through Abby. She had been right. "The speech is going to be televised by CNN, Doctor. All you have to do is turn on the television and listen." She saw Monica's eyes grow hard.

"I would prefer to know ahead of time."

"Why? To prepare some kind of homogenized administration statement denying everything I've got to say? Sorry, that isn't going to happen." Abby rose and picked up her briefcase.

"You know," Monica told her in a brittle voice, "people like you can attract so much attention that the government starts to take an interest in you."

Abby grinned. "What are you going to do? Ransack my office or the SOWF office like the men of the Watergate scandal did? Do your best, Dr. Turner, because nothing on this earth is going to stop me from delivering my speech tomorrow morning." Turning on her heel, she left the impressive office, glanced at the sour-faced secretary outside the door and moved into the hall.

On the way home, Abby felt exhaustion sweep through her. The adrenaline charge that had made her feisty in Monica Turner's office ebbed. She parked her car in the garage at the rear of the two-story apartment building and wearily climbed out. The rest of her day would be spent polishing her speech. It would go perfectly, she told herself. It had to.

A SHARP KNOCK AT HER DOOR two hours later stirred Abby from her position on the carpeted floor. She'd spread her U.N. papers across it to make last-minute adjustments to the speech. The windows to her apartment were open, the curtains moving gently from the warm late-May breeze. Dressed in an over-sized long-tailed shirt, the sleeves rolled up to her elbows, and a pair of jeans, she slowly got to her feet.

It was probably Susan wanting to borrow something or drop by for a quick chat.

"Alec!" Abby opened the door and stood there in shock, looking up at his exhausted features. There, dressed in a dark blue business suit, a briefcase in one hand, was Alec. His mouth, once compressed, moved into a softened line.

"I heard that you were losing weight and not getting any sleep," he whispered huskily. Looking at her rumpled but endearing appearance, he nodded. "You have lost weight."

"Oh, Alec!" Abby blindly rushed into his offered embrace, throwing her arms around his neck. "Alec," she murmured, "I never thought I'd see you again...."

He dropped the briefcase in the hall and swept Abby hard against him, kissing her neck, her cheek, and finding her lips. As if reading his mind, she turned her head and he molded his mouth hotly against hers. The scent of her spicy perfume mingled with the velvet of her skin, sending a sharp ache through him. He tangled his hands through her loose, thick hair, unable to get enough of her. He kissed each corner of her smiling mouth, her eyes, nose, and finally found his way back to her wet, parted lips. Gently, ever so gently, he framed her oval face and allowed his fingers to follow the delicate curve of her jaw and throat. She was trembling, and so was he.

"Alec..."

"Shh, *moya edinstvenaya,* feel, don't talk," he whispered, a catch in his voice.

Blindly, Abby met his heated mouth and drowned in the splendor of his returning fire as a man, as someone her heart had never forgotten. Her mind whirled with questions and no answers. How could Alec be here? How? And why?

Gradually, reluctantly, Alec drew away from Abby. Her eyes brimmed with tears that were ready to spill onto her cheeks. Placing several gentle kisses on her lashes, he tasted the salt of her unshed tears on his lips. With his fingers curving along her cheeks, he held her captive, studied her in the muted light of the hall.

"Tim sent me a message two days ago," he told her huskily. "He was worried about you, Abby."

He felt as though he couldn't get enough of her. Just easing her away enough to look down at her made his heart lurch. Her faded blue jeans were loose and her bare feet stuck out from beneath them. Still, he realized how beautiful, how simple Abby really was. Picking up his briefcase and gathering her beneath his arm, he walked her into the apartment and kicked the door closed with his heel of his shoe.

Shakily, Abby pushed her hair away from her face as she watched Alec go over to the couch and set his briefcase down. He shrugged out of the coat and loosened the dark blue tie at his throat. Pressing her hand against her pounding heart, she watched in stunned silence as he came back to where she stood.

When he placed his arms around her, something gave way within her and she melted against his tall, lean frame.

"That's it," Alec whispered, pressing a kiss to her temple, "just rest, Abby. I'll hold you."

She closed her eyes, willing the trembling to stop. She felt so protected, so much at home in Alec's arms, she never wanted to leave. After a while, her hand resting against his chest, she told him, "I never thought I'd see you again.... Oh, God, Alec..."

"I know, I know." His hands caressed her, imbuing her with his strength, his feeling. "You have lost weight. Perhaps four kilos?"

"Ten pounds, I think," Abby muttered. "Susan made me weigh myself a couple of days ago." Then it all began to make sense to Abby. Susan had obviously told Tim about the weight loss and he'd sent a message to Alec. When Abby looked up into his eyes, she thought she could drown in their warm sable depths. "Talk about a conspiracy. Susan and Tim did this."

A slow smile worked its way across his mouth. "Conspiracy? Isn't that an unkind word? They both love you, and they were concerned."

Chastened, Abby nodded. "I've just been burning the candle at both ends, Alec, that's all."

"So I've been told. Tim briefed me on the way over here about all you've accomplished since I left." He led her to the couch and fitted Abby against him. Her head resting on his shoulder, her hand on his chest, she felt like sunlight spilling across him. With a shuddering sigh, he whispered, "I want or need nothing more than you in my arms, Abby."

His words were balm for her raw and torn heart. Alec's heart beat strong and steady beneath her head. "I've missed you," she said, her voice quavering. "I've never missed anyone more than you."

Threading his fingers through her hair, Alec marveled at how the sun's rays made it look as if it were truly on fire. "I go to sleep thinking about you. In my dreams you are with me, did you know that?"

"We must be sharing the same dreams, then," Abby said wryly, the beginnings of a smile on her lips.

Alec heard the amusement in her voice, thankful that she was now over the shock of seeing him at her doorstep. "I was on board the *Udaloy* a week ago when I received a message ordering me to Moscow. My friend, Mikhail Surin had something to do with it, I'm sure. When I got there, Colonel Pavel Surin, his son, an attaché with the Supreme Soviet Ecology Committee, gave me some new and interesting orders."

Abby looked up. "What orders?"

Alec's smile deepened. "He said that the General Secretary himself wanted more direct activity with the International Whaling Commission. Gorbachev sees this as an opportunity to expand *glasnost* by working more closely with those who seek to help the endangered whales." He saw her eyes grow luminous, sparkling with sudden happiness, which he shared. "I'm here on orders to deliver a speech to the U.N., Abby. Right after you've given yours." He glanced at his briefcase. "And I've been working on it furiously. In it I will state my country's wish to continue close cooperation with the international community."

Abby sat up. She could barely believe Alec was here, let alone comprehend what he was saying. To have him in her arms again, to work beside him in the aid of her whales—it was almost more than she dared dream. "This is incredible," she murmured. She captured his hand, his long fingers wrapping around hers. "How long can you stay?"

His smile dissolved. "I only have five days. Colonel Surin could have made it a much shorter stay for me, but he hoped that you and I could go on American television once again."

"This is a dream come true, Alec, in every way."

"For the whales and for us," he agreed softly, lost in the sapphire color of her eyes. "First things first. Let me get into my western clothes and get comfortable." He frowned. "I dislike suits as much as I do my uniform."

"You were born to wear jeans," she said, envisioning how the tight denim would hug his legs. Abby laughed, suddenly giddy with the realization that Alec would be here five whole days.

"And the friends I mailed the jeans to when I returned to the *Udaloy* hoard their pairs, believe me."

Alec looked relaxed and confident as he leaned against the couch. A few dark strands of hair dipped across his forehead, and Abby no longer tried to stop herself from the natural intimacy that had sprung so strongly between them since they'd first met. Gently, she tamed those strands back into place, wildly aware of the smoldering look in his eyes as she touched him.

"The Soviet embassy wants me to stay with them each night I'm here," he told her, reaching out and capturing her hand, then pressing a kiss to the underside of her wrist.

A wonderful frisson of fire leapt up her arm where his lips lightly brushed. Her breath suspended momentarily, she felt herself again go shaky inside with need of Alec. "No...please, can't you talk them into staying with me? I know we have to fly up to New York tomorrow morning, but we'll be back by evening. Please?"

He studied her somberly. "I can probably arrange it with the embassy, but Abby, I'm not sure."

"Sure?" She sizzled beneath his scrutiny, aware as never before that she was a woman.

He held her hand, tracing the outline of each of her fingers as he spoke. "Ever since I met you, I've wanted you in all ways." His eyebrows dipped. "It was torture not to touch you the last time we were together, Abby. Now, seeing you once again, kissing you—" he sighed. "—I don't know if I can control myself if I share the same apartment with you for those nights.''

The ache in her heart multiplied with the heat in her lower body. Abby bit down on her lower lip. A decision hung before her. Alec was giving her a choice. Did she continue to wage a silent battle within herself not to love him with her entire being while he was here or did she abstain?

''I don't want to hurt you,'' Alec whispered, sitting up, placing his hand against her shoulder and caressing the length of her slender neck. ''It's the last thing I want for you.''

With a nod, Abby understood. ''I don't know which kind of pain is worse, Alec, being with you or having you gone.''

His smile was sad. ''I feel the same way.'' He pressed a kiss to her hair and felt her inhale softly.

''But at least if we were together, we'd have the memories when we're apart,'' Abby said.

''They can be both pleasant and painful memories, Abby, because I have to go back to the *Udaloy*.'' Alec shook his head, sorrow in his tone. ''I'm sorry in so many ways for things that are out of our control. If you were a Soviet woman, then things would be very different.''

''Or you an American.''

Gently, he caressed her hair, which glinted with such life in its depths. ''Whatever you decide is right for both of us.''

Feeling as if she were being torn apart, Abby slowly got to her feet. "I've got to think . . . feel my way through this, Alec." By the look in his eyes, she knew he understood, knew he, too, suffered as much. It was a no-win situation.

There was a knock on the door. Inwardly, Abby groaned over the intrusion. She felt bereft as Alec removed his hand from her shoulder. Giving him an apologetic look, she went to answer the door.

Susan smiled meekly. "Hi. I know this is probably a bad time—" she peeked into the apartment, giving Alec a wave, "—but I ran out of milk for Courtney's dinner tonight. Do you have any, Abby?"

"Sure, come on in." Abby couldn't be angry at Susan and surrendered to the reality of the situation. She would have to talk later with Alec.

"Hi, Alec. Welcome back!" Susan said brightly, and went over to the couch.

Abby saw him stand and give Susan a hug of welcome. In the kitchen, she found a quart of milk, but realized she had nothing to offer Alec for dinner. She told Susan when she handed her the milk.

"No problem," Susan said. "I've got some hamburger left over from Courtney's dinner."

"Did I hear hamburgers?" Alec asked hopefully.

Susan laughed. "I can see the McDonald's experience is still strong in his memory. Hold on, I'll be right back."

After Susan had left, Abby glanced at Alec. "I didn't think you wanted rabbit food for dinner tonight."

He shrugged. What he wanted was Abby, but that had to remain her decision, and he didn't want to pressure her into making it. "A fresh salad is healthy for me. Or so some lovely red-haired woman told me."

Feeling heat creep into her cheeks, Abby avoided his smoldering gaze.

He grinned, grateful that color was coming back to her pale cheeks. The haunted look, the look of longing, was still in Abby's huge, beautiful eyes, and Alec felt hopeless. "Anything you cook is made with love. Believe me, your food is far preferable to that aboard the *Udaloy*."

"Isn't that the truth," Abby said, regaining some of her impish spirit once again.

Susan came back with the ground meat and while Abby went to the kitchen to prepare it, Susan remained behind to chat with Alec.

"How are you and Tim getting along?" Alec asked Susan.

"Better and better."

"That's a good sign." Susan looked happier than he'd ever seen her. "A relationship works because of both people, however."

Susan nodded. "No disagreement from me on that account. Still, Tim's an incredible man, Alec. To use one of Abby's words, wonderful."

He grinned and looked toward the kitchen. The pleasant sound of clinking pots and pans came from the room. How many times had he longed to be part of such a scene again? The thought of living with Abby, of sharing her life, struck him deeply, as never before. Susan was giving him a quizzical look, and he tried to gather his strewn thoughts.

"Tim has been instrumental to all of us in uncounted ways," Alec finally said.

"Don't I know it. He's taking Courtney and me on a picnic Saturday afternoon. I finally decided that my weekends are my own, not the firm's time."

"A wise decision." Alec knew that Tim had wanted Susan to begin to live her life a little less in the fast lane of a career. "You're looking very happy, so I know the past month has been good for both of you."

Flushing Susan said, "I'm afraid because I'm so happy, that it will disappear on me. Isn't that silly?"

Alec shook his head and understood Susan's meaning all too clearly in relation to himself and Abby. "In the Soviet Union, we know happiness is not a given, but rather, a gift. Every person steels himself for the inevitable darkness that follows light."

"I think your country is pessimistic by nature," Susan said seriously.

"Not pessimistic, but we are by nature a very resolute people. You have to remember that we have suffered through so much war and repression that our outlook has been shaped by them. We feel it's wiser to expect nothing, that way, we can't be disappointed.

"You don't seem to be that way," Susan noted.

"I'm different in that one way. I believe in hope and dreams."

"Tim says happiness can be worked at and earned. I want to believe him, I really do, but there're parts of me that hang back wondering if he's right."

Alec smiled gently. "Perhaps you have a soul of a Russian, after all, Susan. Don't let it stop you from being happy with Tim."

"I'm giving it my best shot," she promised. "I'm overstaying my welcome. You two deserve some private time together. Let me say goodbye to Abby. I'll see you later. Enjoy the hamburger, Alec."

He smiled and gave her a small bow. "Thank you."

Abby looked up from her preparations when Susan entered the kitchen.

"Gotta run," Susan told her, and lifted her hand in farewell.

"Thanks, Susan. See you."

Wandering into the kitchen after quiet settled back into the apartment, Alec put his hands in his pockets and leaned against the kitchen counter, close to where Abby was working. A stray strand of hair dipped across her eyes, and he reached over to capture it. Taking the strand, he placed it behind her ear.

"Thanks," she said, smiling at him. "You're awfully handy to have around."

Relaxation flowed through Alec. "Things just naturally happen between two people who like each other," he said huskily. He saw Abby's eyes widen momentarily, and then she went back to making the hamburger patties.

"It's a nice feeling," Abby admitted. She placed the patties in the heated skillet and put the lid on it. Her skin prickled deliciously, and Abby realized Alec was watching her as she set the table for their meal. While she fixed some broccoli to steam, she told him about her meeting with Dr. Turner.

"I think the pressure you've been able to keep on the administration is working," Alec told her.

"I didn't take kindly to her threats."

"No, I wouldn't, either." He grinned suddenly. "She'd be a good KGB agent. They're always trying things like this to pressure people into doing what they want them to do."

Abby put the cups and saucers on the pink linen tablecloth. "She'd be thrilled to hear that."

"Well, when we both deliver our speeches and the press finds out that the Soviet Union is actively backing your efforts, she's going to be unhappy."

The need to hold Abby, to love her with all the fire and passion that she lived life with, coursed through Alec. But he forced himself to remain where he was standing. Before long, he would know Abby's decision. Never had he wanted to love a woman more than her. Never had he needed a woman more than her.

The joy Abby felt dissolved beneath Alec's hungry inspection of her. Suddenly, she felt trembly inside again, as she always did when he kissed her. She'd never met a man who could show her so eloquently through just a torrid, heated look what he wanted to share with her. She knew she had to make a decision—soon. Her heart warred with her head. Love Alec now and take the five days and run with it, or deny herself and him what they both wanted—needed.

Chapter Ten

"You've barely eaten a thing," Alec observed gently as he gave Abby a distressed look. The salad she'd prepared for herself was barely touched. Unlike her, Alec had eaten as if starved, consuming four hamburgers, a huge mound of mashed potatoes and steamed broccoli.

Abby frowned and nervously fingered her fork. "I know."

He took the utensil out of her hand. "Let's go to your garden and talk," he suggested rising.

Abby nodded, barely able to think, her heart screaming at him to stay with her the next five days. Some of the tension eased as he placed his arm around her shoulders, drew her near and walked her toward the small backyard. With a sigh, she leaned her head against him and allowed him to open the sliding screen door.

Alec bypassed the patio and the glass-topped picnic table, and went straight to the lawn, instead. All around them were colorful petunias and marigolds that Abby had planted two weeks ago. They made the drab six-foot-tall pine fence look brighter and prettier, in her opinion.

"Now," Alec said huskily, draping his arms around her shoulders and pulling her closer, "tell me what you're feeling and thinking. You're so tense." He pressed a kiss on her forehead.

A sigh shuddered through Abby, and she closed her eyes. "I want you to stay with me, Alec." Her voice became a strained whisper as she watched his eyes narrow upon her.

His heart leapt hard in his chest, once, to underscore the tremulous words she'd spoken. "Are you sure?"

"I'm not sure of anything anymore. My professional life is at an all-time high, but my personal life...well, I thought I knew what I wanted...now I don't."

The anguish in her voice and eyes shattered him. Alec eased away from her and captured her hand; her fingers were damp and cool. "There are no easy answers with us."

"I can't concentrate anymore, Alec. All I can think about is us...you."

"I can't, either." He gave her a soft smile. "What is the axiom I heard Tim say one day? 'It is better to have loved and lost than never loved at all.' I think it's a good saying, Abby." As he saw a new life light her eyes, his hand tightened around hers. "Come here," he whispered.

Abby came without hesitation. She moved into his embrace, filling his heart as she wrapped her arms around his neck.

"Five days is better than nothing," Alec said unsteadily. "For us, they are the world." He took her hand and they slowly walked through the apartment together. Alec opened the door to Abby's bedroom, light flooding the darkened expanse. Framing her face, forcing her to look at him, he rasped, "I've dreamed about this moment, *moya edinstvenaya.*"

Lost in a haze of joy as his mouth brushed her waiting lips, Abby sighed and surrendered to what she had always known would be her greatest happiness. As Alec's fingers outlined her jaw and he caressed her throat with butterfly kisses, she melted against him and silenced the screaming, logical side of her brain.

"I need you," she said, raising her eyelashes. She felt as if she were beneath his smoldering gaze.

In one motion, he swept Abby into his arms and carried her to the bed. The quilt across it had been made by her mother years before, she had told him during his first visit. It showed three dolphins leaping out of the green-and-blue waves of the ocean. As Alec settled her on the bed and stretched out beside her, he smiled down at her shadowed features. He brushed her hair away from her face until the strands resembled a halo of fire about her head.

"I've been waiting to share a very special poem with you. This is one by Aleksander Pushkin." His hand stilled against her flushed cheek and he was aware of her shallow, ragged breath. The delicious tension stretched palpably between them. He contoured his body against hers as she lay on her back looking up at him.

"I love your poems, Alec."

"Poems are part of the Russian soul," he whispered, leaning down, creating a path of small kisses from her temple to her lips. "'I remember the wonderful moment: / You appeared before me / Like a fleeting vision / Like a spirit of pure beauty. / And my heart beats in ecstasy / And within it are reborn / Divinity and inspiration, / And life, and tears, and love.'"

Abby absorbed his unsteady voice. The words destroyed whatever doubts, whatever fears were left within her. As never before, she realized that the next five days were there for them—for all time. Reaching up, she slid her fingers along the slant of his strong jaw and gently drew him downward until her lips fitted the demanding line of his mouth. Alec was her life, her tears, her love.

The air hung with electricity in the grayness of the night. As Alec slowly unbuttoned her blouse and removed it, Abby felt a sweet, hot tension collect between her thighs. She never wore a bra because her breasts were too small to need support. Every cell in her body screamed for his touch as he lifted his hand to gently cradle her.

"You are," he said in a deep, shaken voice, "so beautiful, so perfect to me."

A sigh escaped Abby as he caressed her, the fire smoldering in her lower body, igniting to torrid, feverish flame beneath his knowing, exploring touch. She wasn't content to lie passively at his side and with trembling fingers, she unbuttoned his shirt and eased it away from his shoulders. How sinewy he was, Abby thought as she ran her fingers across his chest, feeling his muscles tense and leap beneath her exploration. His groan of pleasure made her unconsciously arch against his hard male body.

Minutes dissolved into a melange of color, light, sensation and fragrance for Abby. He removed her jeans, and they formed a crumpled heap with his slacks, later joined by her lingerie. As he stretched his naked body across hers, she realized her sultry dreams of the past month were going to come true. Alec was powerful, filled with tension, and the dark hunger in his eyes promised her so much.

As he leaned down to worship her breast, Abby arched upward, needing his contact, needing him. A little cry escaped her exposed throat as he captured her. She sensed rather than felt him ease her thighs apart, the haze of need overwhelming all her senses, and putting her into a state in which she was only aware of his taut body covering hers.

As his hand slid beneath her hip, Abby's breathing suspended. The next second was like a living eternity stretching before her as she waited for him to fill her with the life of himself. And then he thrust forward, taking her, moving with her until the darkness erupted with explosive lights. Each sleek movement of his body brought her into a hot, fevered rhythm with him. Time dissolved. Everything coherent was lost in the molten awareness of Alec loving her, giving to her until she cried out, clutching his shoulders, and then she returned the gift of herself to him. Seconds later, she felt him tense and strain against her, his groan reverberating through her like a pounding primal drum, their hearts beating in the union of oneness.

He gently brought Abby against him afterward, her head resting in the crook of his shoulder, her arm wrapped across his damp chest. Slightly curled tendrils of her hair clung to her skin and a soft smile lingered on her lips, a smile that told him that he'd satisfied her. Alec felt like crying; he felt like celebrating. Never had he wanted to please a woman more than Abby.

"*Moya dusha,* my soul," he whispered raggedly, placing a kiss on her temple. "You're as molten as the color of your hair you wear so proudly as a banner proclaiming your courage."

Abby slowly opened her eyes and drowned in the velvet sable warmth of his gaze. "I wish I had your words, your beautiful words to tell you how I feel," she said with a sigh.

"You showed me in another, even more important way," Alec assured her, skimming the outline of her torso, hip and thigh. With each caress, she moved unconsciously against him, as if she were a cat being lovingly stroked.

"I feel like I'm floating," Abby whispered, "and I'm so tired...."

Sliding his arm beneath her neck and shoulder, Alec brought her against him. "Then sleep. I'll be here to hold you throughout the night. When you awaken tomorrow morning, I'll be here, too. Sleep...."

ABBY SLOWLY CAME AWAKE, cocooned by a euphoria that made her fight wakefulness and retreat into that wonderful emotional world of sensation and happiness. She had vivid memories of making love with Alec, just as now she was aware of his moist breath against her cheek. She lay against him, one arm and one leg thrown across his sleeping form, her head nestled on his shoulder. The thrill of his arm draped across her waist reminded her that even in sleep he claimed her.

Barely opening her eyes, Abby sighed. She wanted nothing more out of life—the feeling of completeness filled her to overflowing. Nothing could have prepared her for the gift of discovery she made now while Alec slept. Before, in her past relationships, there was still a part of her that had gone untouched. Loving Alec last night had been the most right thing in the world, and Abby knew it now with a clarity that astounded her. With Alec, she felt whole.

Alec stirred, nuzzled his face into her abundant hair and murmured something in Russian. When he opened his eyes enough to realize Abby was in his arms, he awakened. Huge blue eyes filled with flecks of gold smiled back at him in silent greeting. As Abby lifted her hand and smoothed several strands of hair from his brow, he groaned.

"Utro vechera mudrenee," he said, and propped himself up on one elbow, leaned over and claimed her lips. She tasted sweet and hot all at the same time. When her hands slid along his rib cage and reminded him of her sleekness as a woman, Alec smiled against her mouth.

"Whatever you said sounded beautiful," Abby told him, their lips still touching.

Alec felt the living, pulsating tension in her body as she shifted against him in a silent language that dizzied him. "I said 'the morning is wiser than the evening.'" He kissed each corner of her mouth. Easing away just enough to absorb her into his heart, his soul, he whispered, "It's an old Russian saying. It means that things are usually brighter in the morning than they were the night before. I find this to be true." His voice became softer. "Last night, you were torn apart by trying to make a decision about us, about loving each other."

"Not anymore," Abby admitted, running her hand across his prominent collarbone. "I like your

Russian saying. This morning things do look brighter...happier, for me, for us.''

Alec lifted his head. "Want to take a shower together?"

The idea was provocative. Tantalizing. Abby nodded and looked at the clock on the bedstand. "It's only six o'clock. We have time to shower, dress and get ready to catch the plane to New York City at eight."

Alec pulled the sheet aside, revealing her long, willowy body. He caressed her hip. "First, the speech at the U.N., and then we'll have the rest of the time together."

With a chuckle, Abby sat up, her red hair tumbling in wild abandon across her shoulders. "You think the press will leave us alone after those speeches? What an idealist you are."

He stood up and pulled Abby into his arms, her body warm and yielding against him. "And a romantic, don't forget that."

"Yes," Abby murmured, following him into the large bathroom, "you are the most romantic man I've ever met."

"And we'll have time for each other after the speeches, I promise," Alec told her seriously. "*Glasnost* may be foremost, but the Party members at the Soviet embassy are just going to have to put up with me turning down certain engagements in order to be with you instead."

Slipping into his arms, Abby nuzzled his neck and jaw. "I wouldn't want it any other way."

Alec smiled into her eyes. "I wonder what your Dr. Turner will do once she hears our speeches?"

"Probably have a snit," Abby said tartly. "I hope she does." But when Alec's lips met hers again, all thoughts of Monica Turner faded from Abby's mind.

"I CAN'T BELIEVE THIS!" Monica exclaimed at the end of the U.N. speeches. She sat at her desk and glared at the television. "The Soviet Union is siding with that damned woman!"

"Worse," her secretary, Pat, murmured as she shut off the VCR and rewound the tape, "is the fact that several key congressmen Dr. Fielding named are going to push for stronger legislation."

"We've already got two amendments in place! I didn't expect the Soviet Union to give verbal backing to Fielding's syrupy speech. Just who the hell is this Captain Rostov? Some SOWF plant in disguise?"

"I doubt it. You know, with *glasnost* expanding, I think General Secretary Gorbachev wants to be seen as a man who's environmentally sensitive. Remember, he needs all the support from abroad and from as many factions as possible."

"Well," Monica snapped, "he's picked the wrong side on that issue! Just who do they think they are?"

Monica whirled around and looked out the window. She saw nothing of the warm spring morning or the sunlight lacing through cottony white clouds above Washington, D.C. "I'm not going to let Fielding sway my congressmen. I've got them locked up. They've given their word, and they don't dare break it."

The secretary nodded. "Do you want me to call the White House for you? Perhaps a statement is in order?"

"Yes," Monica ground out. "I want to talk to the press secretary. Maybe he'll have some brilliant ideas on how to plug the holes in the dike caused by this latest Fielding maneuver."

"I CAN'T BELIEVE ALL THIS," Abby said as she sat down in the silk-upholstered chair in a small, tastefully appointed room at the U.N. She glanced up at Alec, who stood near the door and smiled. Today, for his speech, he'd worn a dark gray suit, white shirt and red tie. The press had learned that President Reagan was drawn to red and would always choose reporters who wore that color. Now it was the rage: every man wore a red tie, whether he was a member of the press or not. It amazed Abby how some fads got started. On Alec, however, the color complemented his dark good looks.

"Tim's fighting off the hordes of reporters outside this door," Alec said, lifting his thumb and pointing at the entrance.

"Lock it."

He laughed softly. "No, Tim has to escape into here, too. We can't leave him stranded."

"You're right," she muttered. As Alec walked toward her, Abby's shoulders straightened in a confident stance. Alec leaned down, captured her hand and squeezed it and then dropped a gentle kiss upon her lips.

"You were magnificent," he told her.

"And you knocked their socks off, Alec. I saw the delegates' faces." She smiled. "I think they finally realize *glasnost* is for real. It's not some buzzword, it's becoming a reality."

Tim entered the room and quickly shut the door behind him. Dressed in a dark blue suit, he turned and wiped his brow. Although the Coast Guard wasn't involved in an official capacity with Alec's second trip to the U.S., Tim had requested leave and gotten it. He had agreed to act as Alec's press aid to help sort out invitations to various talk shows.

Abby missed seeing him in his uniform, but understood that he couldn't wear it under the circumstances. If he had, the Coast Guard might have looked as if it were condoning Alec's speech and visit.

"Whew, you two really know how to stir up a hornet's nest, you know that?" Tim lifted the notepad held in his left hand. "I've got you lined up for two television appearances, ten radio interviews interspersed through the next four days, and get this—

you'll appear with Larry King on CNN. That's one show that can really get the message out on your whale and dolphin dilemma. Besides, I like King. He's a fair interviewer. He'll give you time to tell your side and not cut you to ribbons. Isn't that great?''

Abby groaned. She glanced up at Alec, who still held her hand. "What was that about five quiet days to spend together after the speeches?"

"I suppose it was idealistic," Alec admitted, a sadness moving through him. "The secretary general will want me to take advantage of the opportunities to help the American public understand that *glasnost* is genuine. We'll still get some time together, though," he promised her.

With a grin, Tim halted in front of them and flipped through the dates, interview times and other pertinent information. "I like *glasnost*. It means the end of the Cold War, and everybody can start putting away their weapons and hardware."

"Amen to that," Abby said with feeling. "If we can get people's attention away from the threat of nuclear war and get their focus on the real problem, our dying Earth, then maybe we can make some real progress."

Somberly, Alec agreed. "*Perestroika* has to work in the Soviet Union, too. It's being viewed with distrust by the people. I just hope they can believe in what the secretary-general has put into motion. It will mean a lot of hardship and even more sacrifice on everyone."

"You're going from a state-supported economy to a free-market economy," Tim pointed out, sitting down. "It's going to take time, Alec, and a lot of painful decisions. I hope the U.S. gives the Soviet Union the backing it's going to need as that shift takes place. Otherwise, I really think there could be riots and strikes."

With a groan, Alec murmured, "I hope not! That would shatter the delicate situation that exists over there."

"No growth comes without birthing pains," Tim reminded him. "Can you tell I studied economics?"

Abby made a face. "No kidding, Tim. Do you have any *good* news for us? First, you tell us we'll have no time together, then you tell Alec his country is going to have strikes and riots."

The officer scratched his head and gave them a sheepish grin. "Sorry. Normally, I'm the epitome of positive thinking."

"You're a nice balance between the two," Alec said in his defense. "I know my country is going to go through many kinds of growing pains."

Abby sat there, content to have Alec's hand resting on her shoulder. For a moment, her idealistic-dreamer side took over. What would it be like to be married to Alec and have him living in her country with both of them working for SOWF objectives regarding the whales and dolphins? With a little sigh, she knew it was a silly dream. But being around Alec encouraged her to dream. For him, the world was shaped by what one dreamed. A spasm of pain made her heart ache. In four more days, Alec was going to be gone—forever.

"How are you and Susan getting along?" Alec asked Tim.

Tim smiled briefly as he consulted his notes. "It looks good, real good, Alec."

"And how is Courtney responding to you?"

Tim glanced up, his voice softening. "She's coming around."

Abby shook her head. "You're so cautious, Tim! Courtney loves him to death, Alec. She can hardly wait until he visits. She climbs into his lap, wants to play horsey with him and chatters away." Smiling at the man, Abby said, "As usual, Tim has charmed Courtney into liking him."

Blushing, Tim laughed. "Now, Abby, that's not true. Courtney trusts me, and that's even more important." His smile slipped. "I just hope I never disappoint her. There's a lot of fine lines to walk with that kid. After Susan told me what happened to Courtney, I cried."

Alec nodded. "A child is innocent. For any man to abuse a child is a crime in my eyes."

The look on Tim's face convinced Abby that if he ever ran into Susan's ex-husband, the man was going to be lucky to escape alive. Rarely had she seen the

Coast Guard officer's hard, military side, but she saw it in the flash of his eyes right then.

"Susan's been hurt, too," Tim told them. "I've been trying to convince her to get therapy, to get some form of help."

Abby stirred from her chair. "I think your persuasion is going to work. Susan told me she's made an appointment with a woman therapist." She saw the surprise and then gratefulness mirrored in Tim's face.

"That's good news," he whispered. "I came out of a family where none of that happened. When she started telling me all this stuff, I felt like she was making it all up, but I knew she wasn't."

"I came out of a good home, too," Abby said, "so I understand what you mean."

"Without Susan getting help," Alec said, "your relationship with her was going to continue to be difficult."

Tim nodded grimly. "Don't I know it. I can only do so much, but, hell, I don't have the experience to give her all the help she needs. It's damned frustrating."

Abby got up and went to Tim. She leaned down and patted his shoulder. "Listen, you've been of more help to those two than you'll ever know. You've given them love, Tim, and hope for a future that doesn't have to mirror the past. That's a beautiful gift, don't you think?"

"I never looked at it that way," Tim admitted somberly. "Sometimes, I just feel so helpless when Susan starts reacting to me as if I'm her ex-husband. I'm not. I'm me."

"One day, she'll see you, not her past."

Flashing a smile up at her, Tim gripped her hand. "Anyone ever tell you, Dr. Fielding, that you're good medicine for whales *and* people?"

Alec smiled as he stood apart from them, hands in the pockets of his slacks. A sadness gripped his heart, and he felt like crying out in frustration and loss. His time with Abby was going to be severely limited by the number of public appointments. Looking down at his highly polished black shoes, he surrendered to his larger responsibility, to *glasnost,* to a world moving toward peace. Like the rest of the Soviet people, Alec realized that personal needs would have to be sacrificed for the betterment of his country.

Lifting his head, he absorbed Abby's glowing features into his heart. How beautiful she looked in her business suit. Her luxurious red hair was tamed into a chignon at the nape of her slender neck, but beneath the conservative business appearance he was able to see the molten, responsive women inside those clothes. His body responded hotly to what he saw.

Alec assimilated another truth. He was falling in love with Abby. There was no mistake about it: he loved her. Last night, watching her wrestle with the monumental decision, he'd cried inwardly for her.

Alec knew he could never tell Abby how he felt about her. It would only make their inevitable parting just that much more wrenching. He didn't want to be the one to put Abby's passion for life, her verve and fire, to the ultimate test.

Chapter Eleven

Abby stirred in Alec's arms. Automatically, he held her a little more tightly against him, her hair a wonderful silken carpet across his shoulder and chest. The bedroom window was open, the light blue sheer curtains moving briefly as the June dawn began to light the sky. The odor of freshly mowed lawn from the night before and the fragrance of honeysuckle blooming along the apartment wall filled the room. He lay there, absorbing Abby's warm, yielding length against him and tried to brand it into his memory, his senses. Glancing at the clock on the bedstand, he realized that in three more hours he'd be gone, out of her life forever.

Unconsciously, he ran his fingers slowly up and down her shoulder and upper arm. When he became aware that his breathing was synchronized with hers, he smiled. How well they complemented each other. The warmth of her as a woman, the perfume of her skin, all evoked powerful emotions within him. He would never be able to lie like this with her again.

His brows knit into a scowl as he studied the pale blue ceiling in the dawn light. Colonel Surin had made it clear that Alec's mission to the U.N. had been an unusual one, and that Alec should not expect any special favors upon his return. That mean that he'd be shipped out to the *Udaloy* shortly after his arrival in Moscow. That didn't bother Alec, because his love of the sea had been a constant, despite the harsh life aboard Soviet naval vessels.

Picking up a strand of Abby's hair, Alec studied it in the burgeoning light and marveled at its beauty, the color a combination of copper, crimson and gold. Her hair reflected the many facets of Abby to him. She was such an impulsive, spontaneous creature, given to the moment. Making love to her late last night had been like scorching summer heat that had melted them into one. His body thrummed with awakening memory of her passion, her commitment to him.

The strand of hair curled gently around his fingers. Abby had done the same thing with his heart: curled herself gently around him. How was he going to live without her? Without her winsome smile, those freckled cheeks blanketed with blush, and her childlike laughter?

It hurt to breathe. It hurt to feel. The woman in his arms, whose heart was as large as the world for those things she deemed important, was going to be lost to him.

Abby stirred briefly, but remained asleep. Alec eased up on his elbow and gently brushed several strands of hair away from her cheek. How beautiful in sleep she was, he mused, grazing her skin. There was such a fierce fire of life in Abby. She was a modern-day Joan of Arc, a member of a small but vocal group who wanted something better for the children of the world. A smile tugged softly at his mouth as he leaned down and kissed her temple.

When had he fallen in love with Abby? Alec didn't know, didn't care. It had happened, and that was what was important. As he looked at her, he thought of the Polaroid photos of Abby that Tim had given him several days ago. Alec knew Tim was no stranger to being at sea; he'd commanded an eighty-two-foot Coast Guard cutter out of San Pedro, California. Long days at sea created homesickness for loved ones, and Tim knew that better than most, so he'd given Alec the precious gift of the photos. Tim was more than a liaison in Alec's eyes. He was a friend. A good friend.

Whispering her name, Alec watched Abby slowly stir and awaken. He placed a series of warming, welcoming kisses upon her cheek and finally, on her lips. His heart burst with joy as her mouth opened beneath his and shared her heart with him. There was such trust between them, Alec marveled as he felt

Abby's arm slowly lift and then slide around his neck and pull him down upon her.

The dawn light dissolved in the gentle exploration Alec initiated with Abby. Each touch, each kiss, became more important, more necessary to remember and place in the vaults of his heart than ever before. Her glorious blue eyes shimmered with tears as he made slow, exquisite love with her until they fell exhausted and sated into each other's arms afterward.

Abby snuggled close to Alec, weak with pleasure. His arms, strong and protective, came around her, and she sighed. The words *I love you* threatened to tear from her. She struggled to hold them back because she knew it would do nothing but make their parting even more difficult. Instead, she told him, "All my life I've believed in meeting head-on whatever was thrown at me. But this morning, I'm a coward, Alec. I didn't want last night to end. And I didn't want today to begin."

"I understand," he rasped, pressing her head against his chest and tunneling his fingers through her silky mass of hair. "And you've never been a coward, Abby. Not ever." He kissed her hair and inhaled the musky, sweet fragrance that was only Abby. "We're allowed to be frightened and scared right now. To deny it would deny what we've become to each other over the past few months."

Abby nodded. How simple, how realistic Alec could become when necessary. "Is that your Russian heritage, the stoic acceptance of the future, speaking?''

He chuckled and caressed her damp cheek. ''I'm sure it is. My people have suffered so badly in our history that we know how to suffer in eloquent, anguished silence.''

Abby raised up one arm and dissolved beneath Alec's dark brown eyes which were alive with warmth for her alone. ''I wish I had a little of your graceful acceptance.'' She sat up and the pink floral sheet settled around her hips. ''My American generation has had more given to them than any other. What I'm discovering is, I can't handle defeat or setbacks like the older generations can.''

''Perhaps the parents of this country overindulged you as children.''

With a sad smile, Abby agreed. ''We had everything handed to us on a silver platter and like thieves, we greedily took everything and ran away with it. We weren't taught to share, to leave a little on that platter for someone else. Many of my generation don't know hardship, Alec. We didn't have wars or face the same deprivation and challenges our parents did which fostered internal courage and the strength with which to face adversity. We just don't have the strength of past generations, and that worries me. I'm having trouble handling your leaving.''

''Our parting is a hardship,'' Alec whispered. Sliding his hand down her arm, he smiled over at her.

"I'm betting that your red hair has given you a genetic courage that your parents passed on to you."

"Well," she quavered, "I'm going to need every ounce of strength I can find."

Whispering her name, Alec pulled her back into his arms. The tears in her eyes tore at him. How badly he wanted to tell Abby of his growing love for her, of the dreams he had of a future with her that could never be. As she settled beside him, he gently splayed his hands across her softly rounded belly. Abby would be a wonderful mother, and more than anything, Alec wanted her to have his children.

But they were dreams, broken dreams that were half formed by the wishful thinking of a heart that until this moment, had been barren. Alec struggled with the realization that those dreams would never come true. Drawing in a ragged breath, he kissed her deeply, feeling her fiery response, her passion coupled with desperation. The hours were falling away, dissolving beneath the harsh reality that he had to get up, shower and dress. He drowned one last time in the beauty, the fire and passion of the woman he loved more than life itself—because she had become his life. The Russian poet Baratynsky had been right about love being a sweet poison, but he was also poignantly correct about love opening Alec's soul. Alec would never be sorry for loving Abby because she had touched his soul and brought life to him.

ABBY SWALLOWED HARD AND slowed her pace down the apartment sidewalk. Tim stood waiting by the government car at the curb next to her apartment, his face somber. Alec stood dressed in a dark blue business suit, his arm around her shoulders. The parting was worse than Abby could ever have imagined. She had worn sandals, a short-sleeved cotton blouse of pale lavender and a matching skirt that hung down to her ankles. The June morning was alive with the singing of birds, the sky a pale blue and cloudless. Everything around them shouted of life, of growth, from the colorful petunias bordering the apartment building behind them, to the leaves on the trees along the boulevard.

"Here," Abby whispered to Alec, pulling a gift from the large pocket of her skirt. "This is for you...."

Touched, Alec opened the small white box. Inside was an antique gold-heart locket on a chain. He glanced down at Abby: her lower lip trembled, and she was fighting back the tears. The sight ripped him apart. "What is this?" he asked, holding the chain suspended between them.

"It was my grandmother's, Alec. A long time ago in my country, when a woman wanted to give her heart to a man, she would cut a small lock of her hair and put it inside the locket and give it to him. It's a keepsake, a wonderful way of always having something of the person you...like...near you." She gestured toward the gift. "There's a strand of my hair in there along with a picture of me on one side of the heart and a picture of you on the other. It's old-fashioned, but I like a lot of things from the past.''

Alec carefully opened the locket. There was a color picture of Abby smiling and a small lock of her red hair, carefully curled on the other side on top of his photo. His voice was strained. "I'll cherish your gift as I cherish you," he said, then he swept her uncompromisingly into his arms.

"Oh, Alec," Abby cried softly, clinging to him, never wanting to let him go.

Words were useless. Alec knew time was draining away from them minute by anguished minute. He eased away from her enough to put the locket in the breast pocket of his coat. Gripping Abby by the shoulders, he winced as tears flowed unchecked down her drawn cheeks. Her eyes were marred with such agony that he drew in a broken breath.

"*Moya edinstvenaya,* my only one. You'll always be that to me. Never forget that." He leaned down and kissed her fiercely, giving her his fire, his life, his essence as a parting memory to hold forever in her heart. Tearing his mouth from hers, Alec spun around, blindly heading for the car.

Abby stood on the sidewalk, watching Tim open the door for Alec and then, as the Coast Guard car drove away, she watched Alec's profile disappear from view.

"Abby?"

It was Susan. Abby trembled as she slowly turned to face her best friend. There was such sympathy in Susan's eyes.

"I'm so sorry," Susan whispered, and she came forward, throwing her arms around Abby, holding her tightly. "So sorry...."

"WHERE ARE YOU GOING NOW?" Susan wanted to know as she entered Abby's apartment and looked at the suitcases strewn around the living room floor.

Abby looked up and gave her a strained smile. "Alaska. It's July—time for me to whale-watch in the Bering Sea again. According to my scientist friends in Baja, most of the humpbacks and gray whales left with their calves by early March, so I need to get to Anchorage to work with Captain Stratman aboard the *Argonaut* again."

Susan leaned against the doorjamb. Across the hall, the door to her apartment was open and laughter from Courtney and Tim drifted out. Abby wore a pair of jeans, hiking boots and a white cotton blouse. The color of the blouse matched her pale skin. Worried, Susan asked, "Have you heard from Alec lately?"

"Yes. He's back aboard the *Udaloy*. Nothing new there."

"Maybe you can arrange to meet him on the Bering Sea?"

Abby shook her head. "I doubt it. Alec can't write about military ship movements. The Soviet hierarchy considers that top secret, you know." With a sigh, she pinned her thick mass of hair back with a banana clip so it resembled a horse's mane behind her head. "It would be nice if we could meet, but I don't hope for that kind of thing."

Gently, Susan said, "Abby, are you all right? I know how much you love Alec...."

Abby carried her wardrobe bag to the couch and laid it across the cushions. In a strained voiced filled with surprise she asked, "How do you know I love him?"

Susan closed the door and came over to Abby. "It's been written all over you for as long as you've known Alec."

Rubbing her temple, Abby glanced over at her friend. "I was the last to know it, Susan. I realized it the second time he came here unexpectedly. Then, it was so hard not to tell him I loved him."

"Why didn't you?"

Abby sat on the couch, her hands dangling between her legs. "Why burden him with that knowledge?"

Susan sat next to her and placed an arm around Abby's drooped shoulders. "Why not burden him with it?"

"Because Alec's caught in the vise of what his navy wants him to do. After her returned to Moscow, Alec tried to get a transfer to the Kremlin to work with Colonel Surin, but he was turned down.

After all the wonderful things Alec has done for *glasnost,* you'd think he'd be rewarded!''

"The Soviet Union isn't the United States," Susan agreed glumly.

Anger filtered into Abby's voice as she opened her knapsack, which served as her purse. "They're so backward in so many ways! Alec opened a lot of doors for them. Right now, the SOWF is working at establishing a branch office in Moscow. You'd think his government would have Alec there to help it happen. But no, they put him back on that miserable ship out in the middle of nowhere."

Abby sat there, her hands crumpling the knapsack. Tears stung her eyes. "Dammit, I'm crying again! Look at me, Susan. Ever since Alec left, I've been nothing more than a crybaby!" She searched for a tissue in the pocket of her jeans, found one and dabbed her eyes with it.

Rubbing her shoulder, Susan nodded. "You've got to keep up the hope, Abby. The Soviet Union is undergoing such lightning-fast changes that they may allow Alec to come back here again for more public-relations duties."

Blowing her nose, Abby muttered, "I don't dare hope those kinds of things when it comes to Alec."

"Tim has held out hope for Courtney and me," Susan said softly, hurting for her friend. "Even when things got rough and I started getting scared, he kept the hope alive for all of us. Now look at me—I'm learning new tools in therapy, and I'm able to start differentiating between Tim and Steve. Because Tim had faith, things changed, Abby. I'm a believer in dreams of the future now, believe me." She laughed and held up her hands in a sign of peace. "Me! The yuppie-generation girl who used to work seventy hours a week. Now, I work forty hours instead, have my weekends free to play and I love it! But if Tim hadn't doggedly and patiently been there to point out these things, and if I hadn't had the courage to make those changes, I'd still be on that greed treadmill."

Abby couldn't argue with Susan's logic. "I'm just glad you and Tim have taken the hurdles like you have."

Susan smiled a secret smile. "Guess what?"

"What?"

"He's taking us home to meet his parents in Dallas two weeks from now. I love how old-fashioned he is, Abby. Tim never lost the sense of family or what it means, like many of us did. I'm finding that it's giving me structure and framework to not only get back on my feet, but to stand on my own."

Gripping Susan's hand, Abby forced a smile. "I'm so happy for you and Courtney. You're right, if you hadn't pulled yourself up by your own bootstraps, none of this would have happened. Tim supported your belief you could change for the better."

"I love him, Abby. I love him so much, I hurt inside."

How well Abby knew that feeling. Holding Susan's hand and seeing the fear mixed with joy in her eyes, she understood. "Have you told him that?"

"No...not yet."

"Has he told you he loves you?"

"Yes."

Abby's eyes widened. "He did? When? Why didn't you tell me?"

Shyly, Susan shrugged. "Last evening he told me over dinner. I lost my appetite, Abby. I just sat there with this stupid look on my face. I got scared. Real scared." She smiled a little. "But Tim's taught me about hope. Hope for a better, happier future."

Thrilled, Abby threw her arms around Susan. "Oh, that's wonderful! Just wonderful!" She embraced her friend and then released her. "No one deserves happiness more than you and Courtney."

Gripping Abby's hand, which was cool to her touch, Susan said gently, "And so do you, Abby. Don't give up the love you have for Alec. Just look at me and what's happening because I maintained hope and trust."

Sadly, Abby smiled. "Don't worry, I have all kinds of hope. At night in my dreams, I see Alec. I'm with him in them. When I wake up in the morning, reality drenches me and I try to balance my beautiful inner world of dreams and what I wish could be against the logic of my awake world."

"Just don't give up, Abby. Not ever."

"I won't," she reassured Susan shakily. "With the fall session of Congress convening soon, I'm going to be working very closely with the SOWF lobbyist and certain congressmen who are leaning toward enforcing the whale legislation. I'll be very busy the next six months, believe me. I won't have time to think too much or too long about Alec."

"Next January you go down to Baja for the whale calving, don't you?"

She nodded. "My favorite time of year. I love watching the babies being born in those beautiful turquoise waters. I understand the Soviets are going to allow Dr. Belov, one of their top marine biologists, to join me on board the ship."

"See, all this hard work you and Alec did together earlier this year is paying off."

Abby wanted to be happy about it, but couldn't. The tunnel of grief she was just now starting to come out of had proved a long and tortuous journey alone. The only antidote, if there was such a thing, was working long, hard hours. She had rationalized her extreme measures by telling herself she would have less time to think, to feel about Alec.

Perhaps, going to Anchorage again would help, but Abby knew it was simply going to dredge up all the old feelings, the memories of when she'd first met Alec.

"At least," Susan added, "Dr. Turner resigned from the State Department recently."

Abby shrugged. "Can you imagine giving certain PAC lobbyists preferential treatment on overseas deals? I never did trust her."

"The morals and values of some of our politicians and government officials has sunk to an all-time low. I hear she's taken a teaching position at some college in Montana."

"A good place for her," Abby said. "Out of sight, out of mind. I wish all my enemies would disappear like that, but they won't." She stood. "The man who replaced her probably isn't going to be any different in political attitude than she was. Sometimes," Abby said with a sigh, "I get tired, Susan. Tired of fighting city hall."

Getting to her feet, Susan nodded. "You're tired for a lot of reasons, Abby. It's been a hard year on you so far. But look at what's been accomplished. So much good has come out of it. You're reaching people."

"Yes, but there's so much more I have to do before—"

"What you have to do," Susan interrupted, "is take a break. Relax, for a while. Promise me that before you leave for Anchorage, you'll have lunch with the three of us and just relax."

"Sure." Maybe being with people who had some happiness in their lives would help balance out what was lacking in her own. And maybe going to Alaska would help her heal. Maybe.

"You're awful quiet, Abby," Captain John Stratman said, glancing at her from the helm. Ahead of them in the dusk, the Bering Sea just south of Kodiak Island looked like smooth, flawless glass.

Abby stirred from the bolted-down chair that she sat on, scanning the horizon for the telltale plumes of whales blowing as they surfaced in the ocean. "It's been a quiet week, hasn't it?" On the console in front of her was a copy of *Almost at the End* by Yevgeny Yevfushenko, a popular Russian writer. The book was a collection of prose and poems by a man who was obviously pro-*glasnost*. Abby was reading it because it made her feel closer to Alec. She wanted to better understand the world he lived in. During the quiet moments, she would keep John company on the bridge, read her books and then scan the sea with binoculars, hunting for the pods of whales.

"Humph. It's late October and nary a whaler in sight. I'm gettin' bored," John grumbled.

With a slight smile, Abby rested the heavy binoculars in her lap. "I think the whalers have gotten the message. At least, for this year." Even now, the Bering Sea area was preparing for the coming winter. The whales were turning south to begin their annual five-thousand-mile migration to Baja, Mexico, to spend the winter in the warm lagoon waters and then birth their calves in January and February.

The *Argonaut* slid along the surface, hardly bobbing at all. Abby wondered if it was the calm before the storm. In the pocket of her jeans was Alec's latest letter, a letter that filled her with joy and sadness at the same time. He was now in Kamchatka, on the peninsula, slaving away at a desk job and acting as an assistant to an admiral of the pacific fleet.

"Eh, what about that Soviet captain? Rostov? Heard from him lately?"

"I got a letter from Alec last week just before we sailed, John. He's okay."

"Kinda was hopin' for your sake that we'd meet up with the *Udaloy* out here somewhere."

Abby winced inwardly, the pain in her heart always there every time she thought about Alec. "He's been stationed in Kamchatka, John."

"Moving up in the world, eh? Good for him."

Wryly, she said, "I don't know if anchoring him to land is good or not. He's really unhappy right now." Wasn't she? For the past few months, Abby had hoped to see Alec by chance, somewhere out on the Bering Sea. But everything was working against them seeing each other. Everything.

Scratching his jaw, John angled a look in her direction. "You've changed, you know."

"Oh?" Abby slid off the stool and stretched. She wore her jeans, a pair of sensible deck shoes and a dark green heavy sweater.

"You've never said as much, but I suspected you like the guy an awful lot."

"I love him, but it doesn't do any good, does it?"

"Not much," John agreed in a rumbling voice. He turned the helm a bit, the *Argonaut*'s bow pointing in a more northeasterly direction, toward Anchorage. "Sorry that it hasn't worked out for you two. The SOWF people are happier than hell over all that's happened." He grinned slightly. "I'm sure the whales are, too, but they don't read many newspapers. They keep getting wet."

John's grizzled kind of humor always cheered Abby up. She stood next to him and appreciated the pale pink color reflected off the glassy sea at dusk. "If they did, I'm sure they'd come alongside the *Argonaut* and shake hands with us," she said with a laugh.

Stratman nodded. "Yup, they would. Well, the ice floe is starting to muck up this part of the world and no one will be running a whaling ship around here pretty soon. What's ahead for you?"

"I'm spending November and December in Washington, D.C. My mom will be staying with me at my apartment off and on when her work brings her to town. I'll be helping her out quite a bit, learning the ropes of her trade a little more. I've got a scientific paper in progress that the university is waiting for. I've promised them I'd get it in before I leave for Baja in January."

"So, I imagine your friends will be happy you're coming home for a while."

The gentle rocking motion of the *Argonaut* was always soothing to Abby. As she stood there, feet slightly apart to account for the boat's movement, she smiled fondly. "Did I tell the latest about Susan?"

"The one who fancies that Coast Guard officer who squired you around earlier this year?"

"Same one. Susan just wrote me a letter telling me Tim proposed to her, and she accepted. They're getting married this December, right at Christmas. Isn't that wonderful? That's so romantic."

Stratman nodded. "Marriage is fine for some people, not me."

"You've always been married," Abby teased, "to this boat of yours."

"That's right, and she's been a fine mistress and an uncomplainin' wife."

Chuckling, Abby sat on the stool. "You're such a sexist, John Stratman."

"And you like me despite that."

Abby's mouth stretched into a smile. "You've got finer attributes I love more. I overlook that particular flaw."

He grinned and winked at her. "So you going home to be in Susan's wedding?"

"Yes, I am. I'm going to be her maid of honor."

"Well," John chortled, "just be careful you don't go catching the wedding bouquet when it's thrown. You know what they say, you catch that and you're the next to get married."

With a shake of her head, Abby whispered, "I could catch all the wedding bouquets in the world,

John, and there's only one man I'd even consider
marrying."

"Yeah, and he might as well be in Siberia."

"Might as well," Abby whispered. She grew quiet.
It was two months to Susan's wedding. Two months
in 1987. The year hadn't been kind on anyone, in her
estimation. Especially on October 19, the stock
market's Black Monday. Abby heard the news of the
gigantic crash on the radio. When she got to Anchorage last week, she immediately called Susan to
see how she was doing.

Abby smiled faintly. Although every stock-
brokerage firm in the U.S. had taken a beating from
the plummeting prices, Susan was in relatively good
shape with her clients. Her sense not to allow her
customers to invest in junk bonds had paid off. With
huge amounts of stock being traded over computers
at lightning speed, the market reeled from the impact. Susan had told Abby, without a doubt, that a
lot of people would lose their jobs, brokerage houses
would fold and new laws to control computer selling
would have to be established.

Picking up her book again, Abby settled back in
her seat. John was heading the *Argonaut* back to
Anchorage now, their job in the Bering Sea done for
the season. They'd saved a lot of whales this year,
and it made Abby feel good, even if her heart was
broken by Alec's leaving. Susan had been right after
all: some good had come out of their time together.

Chapter Twelve

"Abby, I'll take care of all your plants for you, I promise." Susan gave her friend a hug and then stepped back. She handed her a large bag of books.

"There's a *Time* magazine in there for you to read on the flight to Baja. Guess who's Man of the Year?"

"Who?"

"Mikhail Gorbachev. Isn't that something?"

It was, but all Abby could think about was the other Soviet citizen she loved.

"And let's see, what else did I put in your CARE package? Oh, yes, several good books—*Indian Country* by Philip Caputo, *Beverly: an Autobiography* by Beverly Sills, and *Bernstein: a Biography* by Joan Peyser. I know your love of the arts and politics, Abby. You can read these books on board the *Seafarer* in your spare time."

"You're the greatest," Abby said, thanking her. She'd always been a voracious reader.

"Oh, and I put in a lunch, too." Susan smiled. "Your favorite, pasta salad."

Italian food had been the rage of the year, and Abby couldn't have been happier about that because it was her favorite kind of food. "It will be a lot better than that yukky airline food. Thanks for saving me from indigestion."

"You're welcome."

Abby smiled and picked up one of her suitcases. Tim, who was dressed in his Coast Guard uniform with his dark blue overcoat, picked up the rest of her luggage. The winter sun was shining brightly into the hallway of the apartment building, strong and welcome to Washington, D.C. Outside, a foot of snow lay on the ground, and the temperature was in the low twenties. It was January, and Abby was leaving to fly to Baja, Mexico, and begin her annual study and videotaping of the gray whales' calving ground.

"Take the two months and *enjoy* yourself down there," Susan admonished as they walked toward the exit. Courtney raced ahead and danced around Tim, who was laughing at her playful antics. In her arms was a Teddy Ruxpin doll, a stuffed bear, one of the fads of last year. It had been Abby's gift to the little girl at Christmas—along with a plush, bright yellow Big Bird toy.

"I love going to Baja. It's a place of joy, Susan. I cry all the time down there. To watch a mother whale give birth is only second to watching a human give birth."

Abby thanked Tim for opening the apartment door and walked through the slush on the sidewalk to Tim and Susan's newly purchased car, a dark blue Toyota Cressida. The sun was mildly warm, but the icy chill of winter hung in the air. The winter had been long and harsh, one of the worst that Abby could recall. She'd used the time constructively, however, and had accomplished all the goals she'd set for herself. She climbed into the front seat and shut the door and rolled down the window.

Susan placed her hand on the window frame. "Heard anything from Alec of late?" she asked as Tim placed the luggage in the trunk.

Abby shook her head. "No."

"I was so hoping that Alec could have attended our wedding."

"It wasn't for Tim's lack of trying," Abby said. Tim had used every tool at his disposal to obtain permission for Alec to attend their wedding. The Soviets had gracefully declined without giving any reason. Abby's hopes of seeing Alec had been dashed—as usual.

Worriedly, Susan touched Abby's shoulder. "I just want you to stop grieving. It's so hard to see you alone, knowing how much you love Alec. And how much he loves you."

"He's never said it in his letters," Abby reminded her softly, the pain widening in the region of her heart. "And I haven't told him how I feel, either. I'll get over him with time, Susan. Don't look so worried."

"Look at you, Abby. You've lost weight, you don't laugh or smile like before. Take care of yourself, huh?" Susan placed a kiss on her cheek. "We'll write, I promise. Get some sun down there and relax. When you come home in April, I want to see you healthy and happy. Understand?"

Abby hugged her friend, then got into the car with Tim. Maybe Susan was right, she thought. Two months at the calving grounds off Baja, the strong, warming sun and the lovely warm waters of the Pacific would be just what she needed. Taking the itinerary out of her purse, she realized that a month after she arrived, a contingent of scientists from various foreign countries, including the Soviet Union, would be coming aboard as observers of the whale-birthing activities. That gave her four weeks to be alone, to allow the whales and ocean to help her get her life back on track and in order.

"ABBY, THE *POLARIS* HAS dropped anchor nearby. Your six visitors are coming on board in about fifteen minutes," Captain Mike Hathaway called from the bridge of the science ship *Seafarer*.

Dressed in a pair of short denim cutoffs and a summery pink blouse, Abby waved that she understood Hathaway's message. She didn't move her eyes from the video camera taping a pod of whales lolling in the distance near the shoreline. One of the mothers was about ready to give birth in the fifteen-foot deep shallows. Several other female members of the pod were gently nudging her, as if to reassure her that everything was going to turn out just fine.

The birth would be recorded with the use of tele-photo camera lenses, and Abby knew she must hurry. There in the San Ignacio Lagoon, the weather was perfect, with barely a breeze to ruffle the surface of the emerald-and-turquoise water. Gulls constantly hovered overhead, hoping for handouts. Their cries serrated the blanket of silence that was always a part of the area. Occasionally whales came to the surface to blow or exhale, the sound carrying far across the lagoon and reaching Abby's ears on board the ship.

Beneath her bare feet, she could feel the rough wood. The *Seafarer,* a two-hundred-foot ocean-going vessel, had been especially outfitted for such scientific expeditions. Its journeys were funded by the National Geographic Society and the World Wildlife Fund, U.S. Although the ship was made mostly of metal, the decks were fashioned from teak, but they needed another coat of varnish soon. The twenty scientists on board shared sea duties. Whether it was mopping the decks, cooking or painting, everyone pitched in and worked as a team. Abby loved it.

Lifting her chin, she saw the *Polaris* had dropped anchor about half a mile away, farther out in the bay, so it wouldn't disturb the one hundred or so whales that eventually gave birth in various parts of the lagoon. Looking up at the skipper of the *Seafarer,* Abby called, "Mike, can you get Paul to meet those guys coming on board? I'm right in the middle of a shoot. The mother's going to birth any minute. As soon as I've got it on tape, I'll go make formal introductions."

He smiled and waved. "You bet. I've got their quarters assigned. As soon as you're done, come aft and press the flesh," he said with a chuckle.

"No problem. Thanks!" Abby eagerly returned to the video camera set up on an aluminum tripod. The salt air was invigorating, and she inhaled it deeply. The past four weeks had begun to erase the darkness that had been with her since Alec's leaving, and she was regaining her weight once again. Not only that, but she resembled a coffee bean, tanned golden brown by the hot Mexican sun. Her limbs were slender and strong because of all the exercise and her shared duties aboard the *Seafarer.* Abby actually felt as if she were thriving. The beauty of being able to watch the whales birth only increased her newfound happiness.

She heard the Zodiac bearing the foreign scientists drawing near. She frowned, hoping that the sound of the small motor wouldn't disturb the whale mother in the distance. A huge, shining dark gray tail lifted up and out of the shallows, and Abby focused all her attention on the birth. Her fellow scientists would be taken aboard on the opposite side of the *Seafarer* from where she was taping, shown to their quarters and made comfortable. She'd have plenty of time to make introductions and welcome them aboard later. What was most important was recording the calving.

ALEC WAS FROWNING AS HE STEPPED on board the *Seafarer,* the last of six men to leave the Zodiac. At the top of the steel-grate ladder, he turned to a short man with a beard and thick glasses. The name tag on his shirt read, Paul Scotti, *National Geographic* Photographer.

"Excuse me, can you tell me where Dr. Fielding is? Wasn't she supposed to meet us?" he asked.

"Abby will be a little late." The man pointed across the ship. "She's over on the port side now, in the middle of a shoot. There's a gray whale mother calving, and Abby asked me to greet all of you. She'll be over to welcome you on board as soon as the whale's given birth, Captain Rostov."

The sun was blistering hot and Alec wished for the hundredth time that he could climb out of his dress white summer uniform and take the heavy hat off his head. Sweat beaded on his upper lip and brow. His heart picked up the beat once again at Scotti's explanation. "But she is on board?"

"Sure is. Let me show you to your cabin below deck, Captain. I'm sure Dr. Fielding will be with you, soon."

Torn between going directly to Abby and following the friendly photographer's advice, Alec decided upon the latter. He didn't want to suddenly walk back into Abby's life when she was taping an important event for the world to see. No, he'd waited this long, a few more minutes, even half an hour, wasn't going to matter.

Just as they rounded the fantail and approached the hatch that led down to the cabins, Alec saw someone with red hair racing down the opposite side of the ship. His heart soared. Abby! She was obviously hurrying to meet the scientific group. The five men accompanying him, two Japanese, one German, one Scandinavian and one from the Soviet Union, had already gone below.

Everything slowed down to single frames for Alec as he tensely waited for Abby to round the fantail and realize that it was he standing there. She looked like a beautifully long-legged Thoroughbred in his eyes, her limbs golden from the sun, her hair drawn back in a ponytail. Alec suddenly tasted fear as never before. What if Abby didn't love him? What if what he felt for her was only one-sided? She'd never mentioned the word. His body grew taut as she rounded the last obstacle, a huge coil of neatly stacked rope that sat in the middle of the deck.

As Abby lifted her head, Alec heard her give a little cry. She jerked to a halt, her mouth fell agape. Her eyes widened, and the flush of pink that had colored her cheeks instantly disappeared. Alec moved forward, his hand stretched out to catch her in case she fainted from the shock of seeing him.

"Alec!"

He gripped Abby's upper arm as she swayed unsteadily. To hell with decorum. He knew in his official capacity he shouldn't be seen embracing Abby, but he no longer cared.

"Come here," he rasped, pulling her into his arms.

"Oh, my God," she cried, her voice cracking, "You're here! You're really here!" She sank against him.

"It's all right, *moya edinstvenaya,*" Alec whispered in a strained voice, kissing her hair, her temple, her cheek and finally, her waiting mouth. Hungrily, he molded her to him, tasting the salt of the ocean on her lips and the liquid sweetness that was only her. A little moan escaped Abby as she wildly returned his fevered kiss, her mouth wreaking havoc, spreading fire throughout his body as she claimed him with equal fervor.

Earth and sky ceased to exist for Abby. She felt the shocking strength and hardness of Alec's body against her own, felt the way her body gave and yielded to him in so many wonderful ways. His mouth devoured hers, and she was consumed by the molten fire, the longing and lonely months without his nearness all melting away. As he framed her face with his trembling hands, she lifted her eyelashes and drowned in the sable fire in his eyes.

"My God," she whispered brokenly, "you're here ... you're really here. How ... ?"

Trying to control himself, Alec looked up. Paul Scotti had wisely left, and they were now alone on the fantail. Alec returned his attention to Abby. Gently caressing her wan cheek, he absorbed the utter happiness he saw in her blue eyes.

"Let's go to your cabin and I'll tell you everything," he said. "There's much to talk about, to share with you."

Abby nodded jerkily. She refused to release Alec for fear she was imagining all of this. Had she been out in the sun too long? Was she suffering from the hallucinations that a sunstroke could create? Dazed, she led him below to her cabin.

Alec removed his hat upon entering, and placed it on a small bureau dresser. Abby sat on her bunk, which was attached to the bulkhead. Off came his uniform blouse and he hung it over the wooden chair at the table where her laptop computer sat. Loosening the black tie at his throat, he unbuttoned the top button of his shirt and then placed the chair opposite of where Abby was sitting.

"Now," he said, as he sat down on the chair, "we can talk. If Dr. Belov wasn't with me, I wouldn't have had to wear this uniform at all."

Abby shook her head and reached out. Instantly, she felt Alec's cool, dry hand around hers. "Is this real? Are you here, or am I going crazy?"

He ached to take her into his arms, to make torrid love with her. Exercising steel control over his hungry urges, he gently cradled her hands as he shifted, their knees barely grazing each other's. "I'm here," he whispered, "and this is real. We're real, Abby."

Shaken, her voice wobbly, "I didn't know you were coming."

"I didn't, either, not until the last moment. I'm sorry I dropped into your life like this." He brushed her cheek. "I didn't mean to shock you."

Abby felt the strength of his hands around hers, his thumbs caressing her flesh as if to try and take her shock away. "How did you get here?"

His smiled disappeared and he held her eyes that sparkled with unshed tears. "You remember I was working for that admiral in Kamchatka last year?"

"Yes."

"By becoming his assistant, I got some leverage to finally get to Moscow on special assignment. My old friend Misha Surin and his son, the colonel, were instrumental in helping to form a permanent Bureau of Oceanography at the Kremlin. Colonel Surin is running the bureau. He's been assigned the best marine biologist in the Soviet Union to work with him on oceanographic concerns and issues."

He leaned down and kissed her hands. "The bureau's reason for coming into being is partly *glasnost* and partly because our own marine scientists, such as Dr. Belov, who has just come aboard the *Seafarer,* can help all endangered ocean species, not just whales. I've been working behind the scenes for the past four month with twenty countries negotiating an agreement to begin studying mankind's pol-

lution of the oceans and the effects it's having on all
life-forms." A slow smile came to his mouth. "Abby,
I've been assigned as the public affairs officer for the
bureau. I'll be working out of the Soviet embassy in
Washington."

She stared at him, going more deeply into shock.

"Abby? Do you understand what all this means?"
Her eyes were dazed, and she didn't answer. "It
means I'll be living in the United States. This all came
about in the past two weeks. I tried to call you, but
Susan told me you were already here in Mexico. I
managed to talk Colonel Surin into letting me escort
Dr. Belov here and to stay with him until his return
to the Soviet Union two months from now."

A deep, ragged sigh pulled from Abby as she digested his words. "You're going to be living in
D.C.?"

"Right now, the Soviet Embassy is searching for
an apartment for me. By the time I leave the *Seafarer,* the apartment will be ready. I will have to fly
to New York often, to meet with U.N. delegates, but
my office will be in the Soviet Embassy itself."

"My God..."

He tried to read her eyes, the varied emotions reflected in them. Fear started to stalk him. Over the
months, had Abby's caring, or possibly love, for him
died? His mouth grew dry. "I know I'm not the best
letter writer. I didn't want to tell you about the bureau for fear that if the idea failed, you would be
disappointed." He reached over, sliding his hand

along her jawline. "And more than anything, I didn't want to hurt you any more than you'd already been hurt by my leaving, Abby."

A shuddering sigh worked through her as he continued to stroke her cheek. "This is a dream," she whispered, closing her eyes, "a dream..."

"A dream come true."

Tears leaked from beneath her eyelids, and Abby tried to brush them away.

"No," Alec said in a hushed voice, "let me kiss your tears away." He moved from the chair to her bunk. Dr. Belov be damned. Alec couldn't wait any longer to claim the woman he loved. "Come here," he told her, "come here and let me love you."

THE GENTLE ROLLING MOTION of the *Seafarer* reminded Abby of a mother rocking her child in her arms. A soft smile pulled at her mouth as she slowly awakened in Alec's warm, strong arms. How long she'd slept after making love with him, she didn't know. She lay the length of Alec, her leg entwined with his, her arm across his flat, hard belly. She could feel the moistness of his breath against her temple, and never had she felt so complete as now.

As the *Seafarer* continued to gently rock, Abby felt Alec stir languidly at her side. She looked up, wanting to watch his face as he awakened. Those rebellious black strands of hair were on his unmarred brow once again. Coming out of sleep, he looked boyish, some of the strain that was always hovered around his mouth and eyes gone. Following her urge, she pushed those strands back into place with her fingers.

Alec slowly opened his eyes. What he saw made his heart contract with such fierce love that he thought it was possible to die from utter happiness. Abby lay beside him, her hair a thick mass of crimson around her head and shoulders. The joy, the utter joy in her dancing, sparkling sapphire eyes sent a ribbon of fierce protectiveness throughout him. This was the woman he wanted for his wife, his mate, for the rest of his life.

Shifting, Alec propped himself on one elbow and settled Abby on her back. Her welcoming smile, the way she slid her arms around his neck and brought him down close enough to kiss him slowly and thoroughly gave him the necessary courage to speak of what lay in his heart.

His gut felt tight. It was fear sitting in his belly. Fear that Abby didn't love him as he loved her. When he spoke, his voice was rasp. "The past seven months have been a special hell," he admitted. "I read a great many poems during that period, and I found that you and I were reflected in many of them. I understood as never before that poetry is one way to try to heal one's self." Alec held her shimmering gaze. "I fell in love with you, Abby. I think, looking back on it, from the moment I saw you through the binoculars from the helicopter." He gave a little shrug. "My love for you hasn't diminished with time, only multiplied. I didn't tell you the last time we were together because I wasn't sure if you loved me. I don't know if you do even now...."

With a stunned little cry, Abby digested his admission. And then she threw her arms around him. "Oh, Alec! I do love you. I've always loved you!"

He rolled onto his back and she fitted beautifully on top of him. "You love me?"

Tears came to her eyes. "With every breath I take."

Whispering her name, Alec wrapped his arms around her, all the tension, all the fear dissolving in that instant. Kissing her eyes, he took away her tears. Kissing her mouth, he shared his fierce need of her, reminding her on another level of just how much he loved her. Her laughter spilled over them as she kissed him eagerly in return.

Laughter bubbled up in Alec and he simply held her after their kiss. "You're mine," he said. "You were always mine."

"Yes, always," Abby murmured, content to remain on top of him, feeling the strength, the hardness of his body against hers.

"Then, when we return to Washington, I will court you properly."

Abby raised her head. There was a glint in Alec's eyes she'd never seen before. It sent warm waves of expectation through her. "Court?"

"In the Soviet Union, a man courts the woman he loves in hope that someday she will consent to marry him."

Drawing in a tremulous breath, Abby stared down at him. A lazy smile tugged at his mouth and confidence gleamed in his eyes. "Court."

"Yes."

"Marry?"

"Yes."

"Oh . . ."

"Marriage is held sacred in my country. We don't live together like you do here in America, Abby. I don't think it proper that we do that. I think we need time to explore and find out about each other. Courting is a good way to do it, don't you think?"

Dizzy with joy, Abby laughed. "I think it's wonderful, Alec! It's just that in this day and age, courting sounds so outdated."

"Old-fashioned," he reminded her archly, running his hands down her long, beautiful back. "And you are old-fashioned by nature. I've seen it many times." He glanced at his uniform blouse. "And if you looked in the breast pocket of my blouse, you'd find the gold locket with your hair inside it. I've kept it with me always."

Touched as never before, Abby nodded. She laid down on Alec, nestling her head on his shoulder, her hand resting at the juncture of his neck and shoulder. "I missed you so much. I never realized what loving and then losing you would do to me."

"Well," he said huskily, "those days are over."

"I just can't believe it, Alec. You're really going to live in the United States."

"For most of the year, yes. I've also got a small apartment in Moscow. There will be times when I'll have to fly there for weeks, or perhaps at the most, a month, at a time." He smiled over at her contented-looking features. "I'm hoping we can arrange our schedules so that you can go with me."

Abby nodded. "We'll work something out."

"And your whales and dolphins will continue to get Soviet backing. Dr. Belov is anxious to meet you. He's our whale expert."

"Those poor scientists probably think I disappeared from the face of the earth!"

Grinning, Alec kissed her. "No, I don't think so.

"Oh?"

"I told them on the way over here that we were engaged to be married and I hadn't seen you in seven months. They might be some of the most brilliant oceanographic scientists in the world, but they are men and they understood without it being said that you weren't going to be available to them very much today. Tomorrow, perhaps, but not today."

Giggling, Abby said, "You're very clever, Captain Rostov. But am I ever glad you are!"

As Alec lay there, Abby warm and alive in his arms, he closed his eyes. "Every day," he promised her, "will be special to us. The thaw between our countries has been more than just words or deeds. *Glasnost* is about all the people of the world."

Abby nodded, touched deeply by his perceptiveness, his innate goodness toward all life. "In a way, we're a symbol of things, good things, to come, Alec."

"Love transcends everything," he promised her thickly, and gently he began to show her in a silent language that transcended foreign tongues and all political barriers what he meant.

HARLEQUIN
American Romance

ABOUT THE AUTHOR

Choosing conservation and environmental issues for her 1980s book came naturally to Eileen Nauman. Like her heroine, Eileen believes strongly that human beings are ''stewards, not owners, of the Earth and all of its relatives,'' and is an active supporter of environmental concerns. This, she reasons, is a result of her Native American heritage—Eileen is part Cherokee.

She began writing when she was fourteen. Since 1982, she has forty fiction books (written under various pseudonyms, including Lindsay McKenna) and two nonfiction books in print. All of them reflect something of her background; either environmental, military (she spent three years in the U.S. Navy as a meteorologist) or pro-woman. Eileen likes to portray strong, capable heroines in a variety of careers who can ''lend a positive image and message to women around the world that they can do and be the very same thing if they choose.''

Eileen Nauman makes her home in Arizona.

H A R L E Q U I N
American Romance®

THE ROMANCE THAT STARTED IT ALL!

For Diane Bauer and Nick Granatelli, the walk down the aisle was a rocky road....

Don't miss the romantic prequel to WITH THIS RING—

I THEE WED
BY ANNE McALLISTER

Harlequin American Romance #387

Let Anne McAllister take you to Cambridge, Massachusetts, to the night when an innocent blind date brought a reluctant Diane Bauer and Nick Granatelli together. For Diane, a smoldering attraction like theirs had only one fate, one future—marriage. The hard part, she learned, was convincing her intended....

Watch for Anne McAllister's I THEE WED, available *now* from Harlequin American Romance.

ITW